1

MIDNIGHT MURDER

Dear Hazel,
There's something important I need to talk to you about...

By the time the mayoral election was announced in Wormwood, I'd all but forgotten about Jesse Heathen's note. When the devil hadn't materialised in town after writing to me out of the blue, I'd assumed that something else had come up and he'd changed his mind, or, better still, fallen into a bottomless chasm. A silent sigh of relief had been breathed.

I should have known that someone like Jesse Heathen was merely waiting for the right moment to make a dramatic return. When I'd first read the letter, I'd imagined that his arrival would bring trouble in its wake, but this time, the trouble arrived before he did.

The residents of Wormwood might have started to imagine that peace had finally returned to the town and that all of the bad things were firmly in the rear view mirror. Perhaps they'd thought that there could be a time soon when they may even refer to their home as *a normal sort of place*.

They were about to get a sharp reminder that it wasn't.

* * *

The cat flap had sprung open one evening in June. A black cat had trotted into the kitchen carrying something in its mouth.

"Mail delivery, Hemlock? I didn't think I would ever see the day when you'd willingly do something helpful…" I'd trailed off at the end of my little speech because my statement had already proved correct. Hemlock would never have done something as helpful as bringing in the post. Therefore, it hadn't been Hemlock. "Hello, Hedge," I'd said, greeting my familiar's brother.

He'd deposited the envelope he'd been carrying at my feet and had looked expectantly up at me with his yellow eyes. "If you're hungry, Hemlock's got a secret stash of cheese strings behind the sofa," I'd told him as I'd picked up the soggy envelope and shaken off some of the saliva. There was a good reason why humans had picked pigeon post over cat mail.

The black cat had trotted off to investigate and I'd been left alone with Jesse Heathen's next communication. The letter inside of the envelope had survived better than its wrapping, but there'd been places where the ink had run and the message had become blurred. I'd frowned and tried to decipher the words that were still legible.

Tonight - Devil's Jumps at five-past-midnight - something

SAGE AND SECRETS

WITCHES OF WORMWOOD MYSTERIES

SILVER NORD
RUBY LOREN

BOOKS IN THE SERIES

Mandrake and a Murder
Vervain and a Victim
Feverfew and False Friends
Belladonna and a Body
Aconite and Accusations
Dittany and a Death
Heliotrope and a Haunting
Sage and Secrets
Patchouli and Problems
Angelica and an Awful End

Prequel: Hemlock and Hedge

important to show you that will blow your - be on time precisely - favourite snacks are salami and - bring a camera.

My frown had only deepened when I'd read the note - which had seemed like a lot of nonsense mingled with demands. Jesse Heathen had wanted to meet me in the middle of Wormwood Forest at a place where I had once found him standing over the body of a murder victim. He'd wanted me to go there at a very specific anti-social hour and to bring a camera - which had been the most intriguing part of all.

Hedge had trotted back out of the living room licking his lips. He'd made a beeline for the cat flap.

"Hey, wait!" I'd called after him. He'd hesitated for a moment, fixing me with a steady yellow gaze that had hinted it wasn't his job to elaborate further on what had been written. "Are you sure you don't want to trade places with Hemlock? I can offer you free board and lodging and a pretty decent moral compass. Perhaps there was a mixup when you were both assigned by whatever magic it is that controls things like that?"

"What is this? Treachery!" Hemlock had shrieked from the stairs he'd just slithered down.

"I wasn't being serious," I'd muttered, keeping my gaze firmly fixed on the ceiling when I'd said it. I hadn't been entirely unserious either.

"I can smell cheese strings. You revealed my special hiding place!" my familiar had continued - apparently focused on a different kind of treachery altogether.

"First of all, it's nice to offer guests a snack, and secondly, cheese strings should really live in the fridge. It's no wonder you can smell them. Perhaps your special hiding place could be behind the yogurt?"

"They need to mature," Hemlock had informed me, as if we'd been talking about a fine wine, not a rubbery milk product that I was pretty sure legally had to refer to itself as 'cheeze' to avoid being sued over misleading labelling.

Hedge had shot me a look that might have contained some sympathy, before he'd gone, leaving me with my drama queen of a cat and the strange note.

I'd bitten my lip. My first instinct had been to tell Sean about it, but I'd known that there was no way he would want me to go wandering around the forest at night without knowing what I was in for. He would have undoubtedly insisted on coming with me because he knew trouble when it reared its ugly head just as well as I did - and this particular trouble would have won first place in an ugly competition.

"I shouldn't go," I'd muttered.

Hemlock had jumped up onto the kitchen table and read the note that his brother had brought. "A man with good taste! Bring me some salami, too!"

"No, it gives you the most horrible breath," I'd informed him with my mind still fixed on this new conundrum. *If I ignore Jesse Heathen, will it keep trouble from knocking at my door?*

"Bring a camera? Are you doing a secret seductive photoshoot?" Hemlock had mused, also not paying attention to me. "Or does he want you to catch someone cheating on his or her partner, so he can use it to blackmail them? That happens all the time on this show I'm watching about these people who move into a house together and start relationships. Then, they sneak around with other people, and their enemies find out and try to use it against them. The sneakiest ones always get to stay in the house the longest," he'd informed me with complete sincerity.

"Reality TV is not actual reality," I'd reminded him for

the hundredth time. "Do you think I should go tonight? The whole thing seems like some sort of set up, doesn't it?" I couldn't believe I'd seriously turned to Hemlock for advice, but my aunts were both staying in Oxford whilst Minerva - the new Witch Council leader - tried to sort out the mess the Witch Council had been left in and return it to operating as it should.

"You should definitely go," Hemlock had said with such conviction that I'd stared at him, waiting for him to share the brilliant justification that I must have missed. "If you're out, I can watch *Battle Of The Has-Beens* with Erebus. We'll stay up late, and I'll bring out those extra mature cheese strings I've been keeping under your mattress for a special occasion."

"So that's where that smell's been coming from," I'd muttered, feeling rather nauseous.

"Run along and see Jesse. If anything goes wrong, you can rely on me to pass on the news of where you went," Hemlock had continued - probably under the impression that he'd been pulling the wool over my eyes and concealing the fact that he'd wanted to have a vacuous evening without me being around to criticise him.

I'd been unable to resist rolling my eyes. If something terrible happened to me, I'd probably be growing mould by the time Hemlock got around to telling someone where I'd gone.

That was how, against my better judgement, I found myself walking towards Wormwood Forest, carrying a camera, at the dead of night. The only way I could reassure myself that this wasn't the stupidest thing I had ever done was the knowledge that I wasn't following Jesse's instructions to the letter. I only hoped it would be enough to derail his plan.

I suppose that's the benefit of spending so much time with

Hemlock, I thought as I walked towards the outskirts of town, where the trees merged with the final few houses. *You know when someone is trying to manipulate you.* I turned right by a telegraph pole to walk up the grassy bank that led to the forest, noting that Wormwood's mayoral candidates were already getting their faces and promises in front of people. The election had been announced, but candidates had yet to officially declare themselves. That hadn't stopped some of them from jumping the gun.

I raised an eyebrow at Ed Brindle - 'Your open and honest next mayor!' He was dressed in a fluorescent jacket emblazoned with the words 'Community Officer' and was flashing a double thumbs up, that only politicians seem to think will convince people that they're totally trustworthy.

"Oh, come on! Surely this goes beyond promotion and into littering?" I complained when I was walking through the trees and discovered that even more posters had been splattered all over them. If there was an environmental candidate running for mayor, they would have Ed Brindle's head.

I looked down at the time on my mobile phone as I walked through the darkness and quickened my pace in response. If I wanted to find out what Jesse was up to, I needed to get a move on. My brilliant ploy revolved around the fact that Jesse had probably named such a specific time for a reason. It seemed logical that something was going to happen at midnight. He wanted me to arrive just afterwards to take photos. That was why I was going to arrive five minutes *before* midnight and find out what he was up to before he even got up to it.

Sometimes, the simplest plans are the cleverest, I thought to myself smugly when the trees eventually cleared and I climbed up the side of the Devil's Jumps. I paused and listened for a moment just before I reached the top, but the only sounds came from the forest below, where leaves swished in an early summer breeze and tawny owls screeched as they pounced on their unfortunate prey. I had got here before Jesse, I was sure of it.

Still feeling smug, I strolled out onto the top of the stony outcrop and tripped over the body that was lying right behind the rock I'd gleefully jumped over in a sudden burst of joy over ruining Jesse's plan. I landed on all fours and came face to face with… a face.

It wasn't attached to the body.

"Oh no… oh no!" I repeated over and over, because my brain wasn't supplying anything better to say. I took a deep breath and slowly pushed myself away from the open, staring eyes of the head that was so horribly separate from the body lying behind it.

After two more calming breaths and silent promises of many cups of *Sereni-Tea* when I got back home, my shock subsided enough for me to take another look at what I'd very literally stumbled upon.

Someone had chopped a man's head off and left him lying on top of the Devil's Jumps.

"Hang on… I know who you are," I said out loud, before a chill ran up my spine when I remembered I was speaking to a severed head. I recognised the man lying on the ground because I'd seen him earlier this evening. Or rather - I'd seen a *picture* of him.

Ed Brindle wouldn't ever become an honest and open mayor for Wormwood. His campaign had been given the chop.

I turned away and paced back and forth over the rocks, my brain whirring into life. Something flashed in the starlight and I frowned at the silver coin my foot had disturbed. Why had Jesse told me to come to this place - and to bring a camera, of all things? Had he been here already and murdered this mayoral candidate, leaving the corpse for me to find and photograph? I suddenly felt very unwell at that thought. What if something terrible had happened in the months he'd been away from town and he'd gone off the rails completely? Why else would he have deliberately asked me to come here to find a mutilated corpse?

"Hazel! How could you?!" Jesse said, appearing over the ridge behind me and immediately spotting the headless man. He covered his mouth with his hands, doing a fairly terrible job of looking horrified.

"How could I?" I repeated back to him, confused by what he was trying to say.

"You've murdered the man I was supposed to be meeting tonight."

2

PAYING THE PRICE

I glanced down at the body and then back up at Jesse's shocked face again. "What? I didn't kill him! You know that! I would never... I mean, why would I? I didn't even know the man. It's not what it looks like." As soon as the words left my mouth, I remembered a time when our roles had been reversed. I knew that Jesse remembered it, too... which was why he was taking this opportunity to get some petty revenge.

"To me, it looks like this unfortunate man came into fatal contact with the sharp edge of a blade," Jesse said, tapping his chin with two fingers and frowning with deep thoughtfulness. "I can't think of many people who would take a stroll through the forest with a giant knife, but I do know someone who can pull weapons out of thin air." He looked expectantly at me.

"You know I had nothing to do with this," I said, unamused by the devil's accusations. Now that my initial shock over the surprise accusation of murder had dissipated, I could see straight through Jesse Heathen's attempts to toy with me.

"I don't know any such thing," he finished with a triumphant smile that was almost luminous in the dark night. He pushed a lock of his dark hair back from his face from where it had come free from his heavily styled look. His amber eyes flashed with dark amusement that only a devil could possibly find in a situation like this one.

"I wouldn't have come here at all, if you hadn't asked me to meet you at this location at an incredibly specific time. If anyone is suspicious, it's you," I pointed out.

"I do remember mentioning a specific time in my note. It was an important time, but…" he checked his flashy silver watch "…you must have arrived early with the intention of putting a stop to my cunning plan before it could get off the ground, although murder was probably overkill. At least tell me you brought the snacks I asked for?"

I ignored his last words. "You wanted me to photograph something. What was your 'cunning plan'?" It was a very bad idea to let Jesse take control of the conversation when you wanted an actual answer to something important.

"Did you know this man was planning to run to become Mayor of Wormwood?" Jesse began, glancing down at the body before returning his gaze to me. "I just didn't think he should get away with it. That's why I reached out to you to make things right and set the record straight for me, too. It's just terrible what he wanted to do. It was borderline criminal. I've left that life behind me. It's in the past, where it can stay forever, as far as I'm concerned…"

"What are you talking about?" I interrupted, sensing that the drama loving devil could probably have said what he was building up to saying in a single sentence.

"I'm talking about the new me," Jesse explained, smiling and striking a pose.

I looked at his trademark black, well-fitted jeans and tailored suit jacket and shirt. "You look the same to me."

Jesse groaned - as if I was the one who wasn't making any sense. "I wanted you to come here to get photographic evidence of one of the candidates in Wormwood's election trying to cheat his way into office. The new me thinks that Wormwood deserves a mayor who isn't trying to hoodwink the town by making a deal with a devil."

"Deal? You were making a deal with him?" I said, picking up on that key word. "I thought we had an understanding that there would be no more deals made in Wormwood." I had been back in Jesse's company for less than two minutes and I was already the most annoyed I'd been since he'd left town.

"I wasn't going to *seal* the deal. I'm a changed man and would never do such a morally questionable thing. Ed contacted me using an old business card I must have given out at some time or another. I met with him out of curiosity, and then I set this meeting up… with no intention of giving him whatever it was he wanted." Jesse crossed his heart and looked sideways at me to see if I was buying this newfound sincerity (I was not). "The reason I sent you the message to meet here at five-past-midnight with a camera was so you could photograph him walking away with a devilish contract in his hand. I thought you could publish it in your local magazine and reveal to the entire town that one of their smug mayoral candidates is not above trying to cheat their way to power. After that shocking announcement, you would explain that the deal was a phoney and I, Jesse Heathen, helped you pull off your brilliant exposé."

"I see," I said, privately thinking that Jesse undoubtedly had an ulterior motive for going to all of this trouble, and I wasn't going to like it. Especially as I already had my suspicions about what that motive might be.

"I just think that Wormwood deserves someone who plays fair for a mayor. It would be a nice change, wouldn't it?" he said in a disarmingly reasonable tone, which only made me worry further. "I wouldn't have asked for any thanks. A photo of me looking disapprovingly at Ed Brindle would have been thanks enough." He looked down at the body on the ground. "I suppose that's not exactly appropriate now." He sighed in such a way that made me think he was not expressing regret over the loss of this man's life, but regret over a missed opportunity. "It would have been a great way to announce my interest in taking the new job opening in town. You could have published the photo under the headline: 'Ex-detective stops devil deal made by cheating candidate - Jesse Heathen was inspired to run for mayor by the shocking incident'. Pretty slick, right? People don't want smarmy do-gooders who claim to be perfect and are inevitably revealed to be hypocrites. I'll start by coming across as repentant for my own past in Wormwood and wanting to make amends. That immediately builds trust and gets people on my side. I'm a reformed character! Someone to be rooting for! I would have really hit that home if we'd caught Ed Brindle tonight. Shame. He was tipped to be one of the front runners." He shrugged. "But, there'll be other opportunities. There always are in politics."

"You can add 'callous and uncaring' to your campaign slogan," I informed him, shooting an apologetic look at the deceased Ed Brindle - who hadn't deserved to die, even if he had been attempting to skew the vote in his favour. I pulled out my mobile phone to call Sean and confess to, not only finding another body, but also willingly walking into a crime scene on Jesse Heathen's say so. It was not going to be a fun conversation.

DCI Sean Admiral answered the phone and I explained everything.

To say he was unhappy would be an understatement.

I hung up and took a deep breath, deciding to distract myself from what had just happened. "Why would you even want to be the Mayor of Wormwood?!"

"Why *wouldn't* I want to be mayor? I like this town! I have happy memories here, and I want to settle down."

"What happy memories in particular?" I asked darkly, before waving a hand. I wasn't sure I actually wanted to know which of the past disasters he'd been involved in, or had brought about, had made Jesse happy. "You could just live here without being the mayor. Try the quiet life," I suggested, fully aware that suggesting a quiet life to Jesse Heathen was like asking a fish if it had considered quitting water.

"I need a purpose in life, Hazel. I had some time to think on my recent trip away, and even though I have lived for a very long time, I've never managed to find anyone who appreciates how great I am. No one is singing my praises."

"How terrible for you," I said sarcastically.

"It's outrageous," Jesse agreed without a trace of self-awareness. "That's why I know I would be a great choice for mayor. Not only do I have the benefit of centuries of experience of doing things the wrong way, I can spot unscrupulous characters a mile off - because I *am* an unscrupulous character! I'm charming, handsome, and I'm someone who understands both sides of the coin that is Wormwood. I've always helped those with magical abilities and those without, which makes me perfect for this job because I never discriminate. I'm great at giving people what they want!"

I felt a headache growing in my temples as Jesse argued his case, like we were having a debate. "Most of the recent troubles in Wormwood have been primarily because of you. The most responsible thing you ever did was to leave town. Perhaps there were a few decent deeds sprinkled in amongst the rest, but a sprinkling does not mean you're a paragon of virtue, and it certainly doesn't mean you should be running for Mayor of Wormwood." I still wasn't entirely sure why Jesse wanted to land the job, but I was sure I'd disapprove of the real reason when I eventually figured out what it was.

"Be honest with me, Hazel. It hasn't all been sunshine, lollipops, and rainbows since I left, has it? Was Wormwood suddenly a chocolate box town, where nothing weird ever happens? Or… did weird things keep happening the same way they always have done, with or without my influence?"

I coughed. "There's definitely been a lull…"

Jesse raised his eyebrows. "I haven't been keeping too close an eye on things, but I did hear that there was a rather serious incident involving a Fright Fair. I also heard a whisper that one of the favourite candidates for Witch Council leader was murdered, and the whole thing hushed up by the hastily ushered in new big boss… who just happens to be your aunt."

"It sounds like you've actually kept a very close eye on things," I observed, perturbed by how up to date Jesse was.

"What can I say? I missed everyone," he replied with a little shrug and a misty look off into the distance.

My heart was touched for a second, before I remembered that Jesse's number one skill was charm and manipulation. It was something devils were naturally gifted at.

He wanted me to feel all warm and fuzzy, so that I wouldn't be angry about him swanning back into town and immediately trying to manipulate his way into power. "You've told me why you think you'd be a good candidate for mayor, but why do you actually want to be mayor? Truly?"

Jesse hesitated before he replied, which would have been a promising sign from a normal person that the question and answer were being considered carefully. "Like I said before… I'm tired of moving around all the time without having any strong ties to anywhere, but the real reason I want to be mayor is because it's a good thing to do - a fresh new leaf to turn over. I know I've got a bad reputation in this town, so I thought that this might be a chance to redeem myself and prove that I can do something constructive with no sneaky behaviour needed."

I cleared my throat.

"With no sneaky behaviour… after the election has taken place," he amended. "Come on! Everyone fights dirty in elections!"

"Some more than others," I agreed.

We both looked down at the horrible fate of Ed Brindle.

I shook my head. Jesse Heathen had to be the only person in the world who could distract from a murder by managing to make it all about him.

I let all of my feelings of anger and annoyance go and instead focused on what was in front of me. Or in this case, what wasn't in front of me.

"There's no weapon," I said, noting that the instrument used to end Ed Brindle's life had not been left behind.

"No footprints either," Jesse contributed, looking down at the solid rock beneath our feet. "That would have been convenient, wouldn't it? Not as good as someone leaving a signed confession behind, but pretty convenient all the same." He kicked a small stone and it skittered off the edge of the rock and down into the forest below.

I had to bite my tongue to keep from complaining about him destroying possible evidence. You had to pick your battles with Jesse. "There are more silver coins," I murmured, seeing the small flashes of metal everywhere now that I was scrutinising the scene of the crime. Most of the coins were focused around where Ed's body had landed, and I wondered if there were more beneath him, or if they'd been scattered afterwards. "The local legend says you only need one silver coin to get the devil to swap something old or broken for something new," I said, remembering the lore that surrounded the Devil's Jumps.

"I can think of a different tale that involves thirty pieces of silver," Jesse commented darkly, tipping his head at the number of coins. We paused to think about that for a moment, wondering if these coins were meant to signify a betrayal. "You know, all of this may have nothing at all to do with the mayoral election. It could just be an unhappy coincidence. I don't even know exactly what it was that Ed Brindle was going to ask me for. When we met the first time, he told me he was still thinking through his options."

"And he didn't mention the election at all?" I asked. Jesse squirmed. We both knew he'd been well aware of Ed Brindle's motivation for making a deal with him. The semantics of the final contract were irrelevant. "Anyway, I'm pretty sure that this has everything to do with the election," I said, kneeling by the head after steeling myself to take a good look at it.

I pointed towards the partially open mouth of Ed Brindle. "That's a campaign poster. I recognise the colours from the ones I saw plastered all over lampposts and trees on my way into the forest," I said, frowning as it occurred to me that the proliferation may have been an intentional move on the part of the murderer - designed to draw someone curious deeper into the woods to investigate.

"Why would it be in his mouth?" Jesse wondered out loud, rubbing his chin and looking far more delighted by this mystery than anyone in the presence of a horribly murdered man should look.

"It could be that someone wanted to make him eat his words," a new voice said. Sean Admiral appeared over the brow of the jumps. He was dressed casually in dark tracksuit trousers and a hoodie. Somehow, he managed to make the ensemble look more uncomfortable than his work clothes, but that could have been due to Jesse's presence. There was a sheen of sweat on his forehead and his breathing was faster than normal. "I ran here from Witchwood," he said by way of explanation. "I thought time might be of the essence."

Something in his tone made me think that he wasn't talking about the crime.

"DCI Admiral, it's been a while," Jesse said, flashing his very white smile again.

"It could have been longer," Sean muttered, growing silent when he looked at the body that I'd called him to report.

"When I arrived, I found Hazel standing over the poor man," Jesse said with no loyalty whatsoever.

"What happened?" Sean asked me without acknowledging the devil.

I filled him in on everything I knew so far - including the missing murder weapon, the coins, the pre-planned deal, and the potential meaning behind the campaign poster shoved inside the victim's mouth. "It might be rivalry within the mayoral race," I said, shooting Jesse a smug look, knowing that suspicion would fall onto him when he confessed that he was part of that race.

Sean shook his head and typed several things into his phone, undoubtedly signalling for backup and sharing his location. The Devil's Jumps was one of the few places where mobile phones functioned fairly reliably in Wormwood. "I don't know who in their right mind would want that job after what the last mayor did. You'd have to be crazy," he said, walking around to check the body from all angles.

"I don't think *crazy* is the right word. This town just needs someone with an excellent vision to step up and take on a fresh challenge," Jesse countered, doing his best to look deep and thoughtful.

Sean looked at him for a long moment. He turned back towards me. "He's running for mayor, isn't he? Who does he think is going to vote for him after all of the trouble he's caused in this town? He'd have to coerce the residents at gunpoint to get a single ballot in his favour."

Jesse looked alarmingly thoughtful when Sean said that.

"If you think he did this, I'll arrest him right now," Sean said, still pretending that Jesse wasn't standing right next to him. "We can build a case against him later. I'm not even against making some of it up."

"Did I hear that you two finally got together? I won't deny you make a cute couple, but it's rather predictable, isn't it? The local interest magazine writer, who can't seem to keep her nose out of trouble, and the local detective, who has to deal with the aftermath of the trouble. Very vanilla. Still, I suppose there are even some people out there who would genuinely choose vanilla as their favourite flavour of ice-cream. Really, really boring people."

"Your offer is tempting," I said to Sean, doing some ignoring of Jesse of my own.

There was a moment of silence again before the DCI

sighed. "I think it might be better if neither of you is here when my backup arrives. To say that your faces have become a familiar sight at crime scenes would be an understatement. Don't leave town," he finished, pointing at Jesse.

"Of course I won't leave town. I've got an election to win."

"Not on my watch," Sean muttered, looking back at the notes he'd made on the little flip pad he carried everywhere. "Actually, Hazel, if you could stay behind for a little longer, that would be great."

"Police are supposed to be politically unbiased," Jesse informed Sean. "Don't try to get in my way, or…"

"…You'll lop my head off?" Sean suggested, raising his eyebrows and daring him to confess to murder. "Why would you even want to be mayor? It doesn't make any sense."

"That's what *I* said!" I told him with a smile.

"I don't have to put up with this," Jesse said, turning to leave.

"Wait!" I yelled, suddenly thinking of something. I rushed over and rifled through his dark suit jacket, before patting down his trousers like I was working for airport security.

"Do you really think I'm hiding a sword down my trousers? That would be either very brave, or very foolish!" Jesse protested.

I pulled out the small folder I'd finally located inside a hidden pocket in the jacket. It was a rather small pocket for a rather large folder, but I knew magic when I saw it. "Devil Deals," I read out loud for everyone's benefit.

"Open it! There's nothing but blank paper inside. I wasn't lying about never intending to make a deal. I didn't bring any contracts with me because I knew that…" he stopped talking and glared at Sean, who'd been about to jump in with a murder accusation "….because I knew that Hazel would think that I was going to make a deal with old Eddie boy and then sell him out for my own personal gain. Therefore, I made sure everything was squeaky clean. I knew you'd search me. I planned to use the folder as a prop, in case you're wondering why I have it at all."

I squinted at the item I was holding and saw no signs of spells of concealment. The folder appeared to be a normal folder.

"See? Just a prop," Jesse said, shoving his hands in his trouser pockets and trying to look like a cool cucumber.

I sighed, not completely certain that he hadn't been hiding a trick or two up his sleeve, but for once, Jesse Heathen was not the biggest problem in the current vicinity. "Okay, you can go," I decided.

"Wait!" Sean interjected, making Jesse roll his eyes. "You are not permitted to discuss what you have witnessed tonight with anyone. An official announcement will be made and key details will be shared then, but the rest must be withheld for the benefit of the investigation. Any unapproved disclosure will result in legal action."

"You must be fun at parties," Jesse said, looking bored. "I'll see you on the campaign trail. Don't forget who to vote for!" He flashed peace signs at us, before striding off the top of the rocky outcrop and heading back into the trees. He was walking in the opposite direction to Wormwood, but I didn't waste too much time wondering about it. Jesse was able to use his devilish powers to travel through shadows if he wanted to.

"Why does he *really* want to be mayor?" Sean said once he was certain that Jesse had gone. The fact that this was the first question to leave his lips when we were standing next to a man without a head - who definitely hadn't died of natural causes - said a lot about how much trouble Jesse was capable of causing.

"I'm sure that's something we'll find out the hard way. What I told you on the phone was everything I know so far. Jesse asked me to come here at a specific time and to bring a camera. I arrived early to catch him out. Instead, I found a body." Sean's grey gaze bored disapprovingly into my own. "I know I shouldn't have come here, but I thought I was going to beat Jesse at his own game. If you were me, wouldn't you have wanted to find out what he was getting up to, rather than sitting at home wondering?"

"Yes, I would have wanted to find out exactly what he was up to… which is why you should have called me," Sean pointed out.

All of a sudden, I realised he was angry - really angry with me. "But then you'd have been the one to find the body and you'd have had to explain what you were doing out here," I countered. Sean's brow knitted more deeply. "I'm sorry," I added, feeling rather strange that my decisions could affect someone else so keenly. I was used to being responsible for myself and it not affecting anyone outside of me - and possibly Hemlock at a stretch, but only because his snack slave might disappear. My aunts cared about me, but we still lived very independent lives. Now that I was in a relationship with Sean, everything was different, and I was still getting used to it. When you were together, the things you did mattered to the other person. I'd just crossed one of the boundaries that I hadn't even known existed.

"Next time Jesse Heathen asks you to do anything remotely suspicious, please let me know before you do it. I know you're capable of handling tough situations, but that man has a way of convincing people to dance to his tune," he said, glaring at the last place we'd seen Jesse.

"I wouldn't worry about that. The only reason he wanted me here was to set up a press opportunity for himself. Now that there's been a murder, he can't take credit for anything - except potentially the murder itself." I bit my lip. "But I don't think he did anything more criminal than setting up the meeting with Ed Brindle."

"Are you sure he didn't want to take his competition out?" Sean asked, but his heart wasn't in it. We both knew that Jesse preferred subtle manoeuvres to a full frontal assault.

I looked back down at Ed Brindle. "It looks like it only took one stroke to, er, separate the parts. That probably took some skill and experience to achieve."

"The pathologist will need to have their say, but it does look like a remarkably clean cut. The killer must have had some talent… or magic," Sean finished, looking questioningly at me.

"There are no traces of magic around here," I informed him, checking again with witch sight, just in case anything had escaped my notice the first time. "If the blade was magically enhanced, it might have left traces behind, but it probably wouldn't… because the magic would be in the weapon itself - not in a spell to harm someone directly," I explained.

Sean sighed. I knew he'd been hoping for a simpler answer. "I suppose I'm going to have to canvas the town to find out if anyone saw someone casually carrying around a sword, an axe, or a machete. Knowing Wormwood, that might be some residents' idea of a normal Friday night. My backup will probably be here soon. I know you said it on the phone, but you definitely didn't know Ed Brindle?" he tacked on.

"I'm sure I've seen him around in passing, but that's about it. It will be hard to find a motive for me to have committed this murder," I added, knowing that Sean was just troubleshooting in preparation for his colleagues' questions when they inevitably discovered that I'd been the one to find the body.

Sean looked a little guilty and nodded. "Well, don't leave town," he said, making a stab at humour.

I smiled, knowing it was a sign that things were going to be okay between us - even though, right now, what was between us was a headless corpse that was definitely not okay. "Good luck," I said, patting him on the arm and giving him an encouraging smile.

He rubbed his face and suddenly looked like he was missing several days' worth sleep. I made a note to ask him what was keeping him up so late when we next had a non-murder related conversation.

"Something tells me I'm going to need it," he said, gloomily.

I left him with a smile, but it fell from my face the moment that I was homeward bound beneath the dark trees. There was a familiar bad feeling in my gut… one which whispered that this was the start of something new and terrible.

Local elections could be cutthroat, but this time, someone had really lost their head.

3

FLABBY FAMILIAR

"One ounce of potato mash, shake up some cola and throw in a splash. Next comes the pepper, stir in a dash… that's the way to cook up some cash!"

I blinked sleep out of my eyes the next morning and glanced at the clock on my bedside table, which displayed an alarmingly late time. Clearly, my years of being an adult were catching up with me because I had not bounced back from the unexpected late night. I swung my legs over the side of the bed and frowned. Hadn't something woken me up?

"Stir it around, cook it up, fill our pockets, change our luck!"

Someone was singing.

I got dressed, having showered last night to try to get the horrible image of Ed Brindle's last moments out of my mind. Then, I made my way downstairs. A large cauldron was balanced on the kitchen table. The things that had previously belonged on the table were scattered all over the floor, which immediately told me the identity of the table clearer. Sure enough, Hemlock was clutching a spoon and leaning over the cauldron whilst he sang at the top of his voice. What I hadn't been expecting was for his voice to be joined by Aunt Linda's.

"I thought you were in Oxford with Minerva?" I said, walking past the pair to turn the kettle on. I searched for a few moments and then picked up a box of my morning teabags, which had a new storage location in the middle of the kitchen floor. Erebus mooched his way over to me and I rubbed his fuzzy, black head, feeding him some dog treats. He shot me a look as if to say: 'I had nothing to do with this' which I fully believed. With Aunt Minerva absent so often, it felt like it was me and my hellhound, Erebus against my supposed familiar and Aunt Linda.

"Minerva sent me back to look after the business. She said that she felt guilty about leaving you with so much responsibility when you should be out having fun. Like right now, for instance! Why don't you go outside and have some fun?" Linda suggested, unsubtly trying to step in front of the cauldron and block it from my view.

I had my doubts that any of what she'd just said had been true. Knowing Aunt Linda, she'd probably done something to get herself sent home and was now taking advantage of the fact that her older, more responsible, sister was otherwise engaged, running the Witch Council. "What are you cooking up in that giant cauldron you're trying to hide?" I asked, not in the mood for games this morning.

"Don't tell her, she'll ruin it!" Hemlock said, apparently forgetting that I was the only one who could understand him. He made eye contact with me and then - slowly and defiantly - he threw the brand new business cards I'd bought to promote my tea inventions into the soupy mess inside the cauldron.

"You little pest!" I said, rushing over in annoyance, before immediately realising it was a lost cause. The goop was turning green before my very eyes and sparkling bubbles burst, releasing a scent that reminded me of sour apple sweets - fake and not entirely appealing.

"Did you and Jesse have a good time last night? You got back *very* late. I bet you got up to some interesting things…" Hemlock said, leaning his furry elbow against the cauldron edge and trying to sound casual about the whole thing.

"Jesse Heathen? That devil is back in town? He is rather handsome," Linda said, continuing to stir the cauldron. "But Sean is far more dependable. Less reckless, but dependable is good… reliable, like an old Volvo driven by a geography teacher. He's probably the best choice for someone like you, Hazel."

"Thanks a bunch!" I said, wondering what I'd done to convince my aunt I was perfect for someone likened to an old and boring car. "For your information, Hemlock, I did not have a good time at all with Jesse, and I certainly didn't go there to have a good time either!" I said, before this nonsense could go any further. "Plus, it turned out to be an even worse time than the bad time I had anticipated!"

"Did he turn you down?" Linda asked, looking crestfallen on my behalf. She gave the cauldron an extra big, sympathetic stir and some of the green goop slopped onto Hemlock's elbow.

"Uh-oh," my cat said, but I was too busy putting the pair straight to focus on him.

"I'm in a relationship with Sean! I'm happy! I only went to see Jesse in order to foil one of his plots, because I knew he was up to no good. It was not a social call. Even less so when I found the body," I added out of exasperation and a strong desire to quell any malicious rumours.

"Body?" Aunt Linda asked and stopped stirring. Hemlock ducked the small tidal wave of green gloop that was unleashed by the sudden halt. The salt and pepper shakers that had previously sat on the table top were not so fortunate. "Anyone we knew?"

"Let's just say that one runner is already out of the mayoral race," I said, before shaking my head. "I'm not supposed to be telling anyone anything about it." Sean hadn't specifically instructed me to stay silent, but it stood to reason that I was subject to the same rules as Jesse, and this morning I was seized by a need to be prickly after the assumptions that had been made about the events of last night. That, and it was nice being the one keeping secrets for once.

"Was it the postman who bit the dust?" Aunt Linda asked.

I frowned and shook my head.

"Shame. I've never liked him. What about that awful traffic warden?"

I was sensing a theme.

"It wasn't someone any of us knew personally. It was just a man who was going to run as a candidate for mayor, but instead, he lost his head," I said, frustrated into sharing the truth.

"Lost his head… in a literal sort of way?" Aunt Linda was wide awake this morning.

"I can't say anything else! I haven't even given an official statement yet. Someone will probably be round any moment to take it," I protested.

"Oh, go on. You can't leave us hanging like this," Aunt Linda wheedled. "I'll cut you in on this spell?"

"I can't believe you went out and had an adventure without me. Headless corpse was on my bucket list!"

Hemlock complained. He was still trying to scrape off the green goop.

"Is that a 'to see' type bucket list, or a 'to do'?" I sought to clarify and was unsurprised when my familiar hesitated and rubbed his chin.

"How do you know he was thinking of running for mayor?" Aunt Linda asked, picking up on every single detail of my deliberately vague story.

I suppressed a sigh. This was not going to plan. "There were posters everywhere, including one upon his person." At least that wasn't going into too much detail. "I think there's a chance that this murder has something to do with the election itself, which is all we need!" I couldn't resist adding.

"I'm amazed anyone from this town would want to run for mayor after everything that's happened. Even if they only half remember what happened with the last mayor, they should still know better. I suppose the power appeals to some, more than others."

"What power? Mayors don't have much power at all! The last one was... an exception to the rule," I said, trying not to think back to what had occurred on Midsummer's Eve, almost one year ago.

"Power, you say?" Hemlock mused, doing so much chin rubbing I wouldn't be surprised if he made himself bald.

There was a small popping sound and the fur covering his elbow turned into copper coins. The sudden weight nearly made him fall off the table, before the few strands of hair left untouched realised they were fighting a losing battle and promptly fell out, leaving his elbow completely bald.

"Gah!" he shrieked at the same moment the salt and pepper shakers became twin pyramids of pound coins.

"I suppose that's why someone who's definitely *not*

from this town wants to run for mayor," I said, ignoring Hemlock's antics.

"You mean Jesse? Jesse wants to run for mayor?" Aunt Linda was on fire today.

"I didn't know that there was going to be an election for a new mayor. I thought we were all happily living in lawless anarchy," Hemlock commented having shrugged off the coin incident and completed a fresh round of chin rubbing and silent plotting.

I looked sideways at him. "We don't live in lawless anarchy. The mayor does not make laws for a town. Mayors just…" I considered for a moment.

"Turn up for photo opportunities?" Linda suggested. "Cut ribbons?"

"Something like that," I mumbled, suddenly realising I didn't actually know the ins and outs of the job. The town's last mayor had definitely not been a good benchmark to judge all mayors by.

"I bet there's still power and legions of people who worship you and have to do what you say. If I was the mayor, I would make the laws," Hemlock decided and was ignored by all of those who could understand him (me).

"Mayor Jesse Heathen. I suppose it does have a ring to it. He'll probably be good for the town's image, because his image is good," Linda said - already deciding the outcome of an election that was yet to even have its candidates officially declared.

"Over my dead body," I said at the same time as someone else.

Sean shut the shop door behind him. "Good morning," he said, the shadows beneath his eyes hinting that the opposite was actually true, and that his morning had probably begun in the forest last night with no sleep interval in-between. "Hazel, officially, you're required to come to

Witchwood Police Station to give a statement about last night. I also need to question you about any relationship you may have had with the deceased and the reason why you were out in the forest at that precise location. Unofficially, I know your terrible reason for being there and your uncanny ability to be in the wrong place at the wrong time, so I suppose I'll have to come up with something that sounds plausible and doesn't mislead anyone else looking into the case. This is going to require a big investigation. It doesn't get more 'cut and dry murder' than a beheading."

"Being stabbed in the back," Aunt Linda said out of the blue.

We all looked at her.

"I just mean that it's at least as cut and dry, if not more so. A beheading could be accidental, but no one stabs themselves in the back."

Sean cleared his throat and looked plaintively at me. He wanted this conversation to be a private one.

He had a better chance of convincing Hemlock to take up knitting.

"I can't believe I didn't know there was going to be an election for mayor!" Hemlock muttered to himself.

"That's because you've spent the last several months vegging out in front of the television and ignoring the outside world. You're getting flabby. Hedge looked lean and mean when he came to visit."

"How dare you!" Hemlock said, before reaching down and giving his belly a little push. "I'm twice the cat Hedge is."

"Quite literally," I sniped, before beckoning to Sean and leading him back into the shop. I could have cast a soundproofing spell, but it seemed rather pointless as I knew my aunt wouldn't let the matter drop unless I told her what was going on. I also thought Sean wasn't here to talk secrets, he just wanted to be able to get a word in edgeways.

"I don't suppose you found any massive clues after I left the scene last night?" I asked, just in case I'd missed something obvious.

Sean shook his head and looked sour. "We've got nothing, no leads at all. The man's family has been informed of what happened, but when we asked if they'd noticed anything strange, or heard Ed talk about feeling threatened, they said they hadn't seen him in quite some time. He's divorced and his children have grown up. He lives a largely solitary life," Sean said, shaking his head. "All I've got to go on is a mayoral manifesto that he'd shared online, and the poster that was shoved in his mouth - which seems to be the only clue there is about the motive for murder. There were coins, too - thirty of them - but I'm not sure what that means, beyond the obvious Biblical reference. The official candidacy announcement event is today. There's a meeting being held in the community college's assembly hall. The idea is that Wormwood residents can come and meet the potential candidates for mayor and informally ask them a few questions, as well as supporting their favourites. All candidates must officially declare today, or at least have their name and running fee put into a special box to be read out by the stand-in mayor, if they are unable to attend in person. If the murder last night does have something to do with the election, then the killer is likely to be in attendance."

"Maybe one of the other candidates really did decide to take out the competition early?" I said, remembering the accusation Sean had wanted to push towards Jesse. That didn't mean it couldn't be true of someone else.

"It's too early to make any judgements yet, but my officers will be attending the event, and I will be announcing

Ed Brindle's death and subsequent withdrawal from the mayoral race when the time is right."

A heavy silence fell as we both thought about what a barrel of laughs that promised to be.

"Maybe we could get some cake at the Bread Cauldron Bakery afterwards?" I suggested. Sean nodded, grateful to have something to look forward to in a day that was likely to be filled with amateur dramatics.

But even with such low expectations, neither of us saw it coming - the moment that would define the election and demonstrate that death was definitely here to stay in Wormwood.

4

CANDIDATES FOR MURDER

"Remind me again why you're here?" I asked Hemlock, who was riding on my shoulder like a parrot. Or in this case, like a very lazy cat.

"Someone accused me of getting flabby. I'm getting out of the house and exercising."

"You're sitting on my shoulder," I pointed out.

"I'm warming up."

I decided not to argue any further. Arguing with Hemlock was akin to repeatedly running into a cactus. It didn't take Sean and me long to reach the community college, which was closed for the weekend. A small crowd of people had gathered outside the front doors. They were chatting cheerfully, and it was only too obvious that news of the new maniacal murderer in town had not yet spread. Jesse had miraculously managed to stay silent.

"Everyone is in plainclothes," Sean said in a low voice when I was on the cusp of asking him where the other police officers were. As soon as he said it, I realised it was the only thing that made sense. The murder had not been publicly announced, and Sean was hoping that the killer would let their guard down - perhaps even believing that no one had reported their dark deed.

"Hey, there's Hedge! Later, losers," Hemlock said, clawing his way down my back and trotting off after the disappearing black shape of his brother.

Sean frowned after him. "Is your cat sucking his stomach in? I didn't think cats could do that."

"I told him he was getting flabby," I confessed. "If Hedge is here, that probably means Jesse was serious about running for mayor." Part of me had hoped he'd been saying it to wind me up (which had been hugely successful) but it would appear that he'd meant what he'd said. I looked around, but I couldn't see Jesse anywhere, which probably meant he was planning an exceedingly tiresome dramatic entrance. "At least Hemlock's with Hedge, so he won't be able to mess anything up," I said - like the naive fool I was.

When the hour struck eleven, the doors opened and all of the loitering people filed into the building and made their way to the hall. Sean hesitated for a moment longer, straightening his tie as he steeled himself for all that was to come, before we followed them inside.

"Keep your eyes open," he said to me. I knew saying something so obvious was just his way of calming his nerves. I hadn't been intending to put on a blindfold at any point during proceedings.

"Good morning everyone," a woman with a face like a bowlful of bread dough said from the podium that had been set up on the stage at the front of the hall. When the audience largely ignored her and kept chatting, she tapped the microphone until a squeal of feedback shrieked through the speakers. "Good morning!" she repeated in a far louder voice. There were murmurs and a few goody-two-shoes answered 'good morning' back in a chorus, like this was a school assembly instead of a political event.

The woman pushed her red winged spectacles further up her nose and shook out her mouse-coloured pageboy cut, pleased that people were now listening to her. On the projector screen behind her, the town crest with its seven rampant black cats flashed up with the words 'Wormwood Mayoral Election' written below.

"That's the stand-in mayor, Anita Heron. I had a word with her on the phone this morning to go through the event schedule and prepare her for my announcement," Sean said into my ear. "She's going to bring the candidates in, and when everyone running for mayor has been introduced, I will make a statement about Ed Brindle."

His voice tickled me, and for one moment of madness, I discovered my thoughts were far away from murder and hyper focused on the man sitting next to me on the metal and cushion chairs. He smelled of sandalwood and the sea.

"Clever… that way we'll get to see everyone and witness their reactions," I observed.

"It's been my pleasure to stand-in as Mayor of Wormwood over the past several months, as was my duty as a local council representative. However, the time has come to pass the baton on to someone who will help Wormwood to become an even happier, friendlier little town than it is now," Anita Heron continued, beaming around.

"Is she living in a different town?" I said out of the corner of my mouth.

"I told her to act as if everything is normal, but that's probably too normal for here," Sean whispered back.

Anita cleared her throat when the muttering became a silence instead of the applause she'd apparently anticipated after those stirring words. "Without further ado, it's time for the candidates to introduce themselves to all of you, state why they are running for mayor, and share a few things about themselves." This time, a smattering of applause did follow her words. The audience was relieved that the show was finally getting underway.

It's probably a good thing she's not running to be mayor, I silently observed, but I didn't say it out loud because words could do as much harm as misused magic.

A man in his forties with golden-brown hair that was long enough to scrape his chin and skin that looked like it had been tanned doing exciting outdoor activities in countries blessed with much better weather than the UK approached the podium. He paused to smile around at the room with his blue eyes crinkling at the corners. "Looks like I'm the first to bite the bullet," he said. There were polite laughs. "I'm Andy Carat. I moved to Wormwood from Witchwood a few years ago with my lovely wife. Since then, I've seen the town go through changes, both good and bad. I know there are candidates here today who have lived in Wormwood their whole lives, but it's my belief that sometimes a change is exactly what's needed for a place that might have become a little bit stuck in the mud in recent times." He paused, taking the microphone off its stand and walking slowly and deliberately across the stage.

"I own a classic car - a Chevrolet Bel Air that was given to me by my father right after I passed my test when I was a teenager. It was the last gift he ever gave me, may he rest in peace. The thing with classic cars is you don't want to change anything about them. You can replace the parts with original parts from other cars of the same model, and that helps keep the old girl running. But what happens when there's a problem you can't fix, like rust eating away at the paintwork?" He hesitated again, knowing that he had the audience in the palm of his hand. "That's when you've got to take a risk and make a drastic change. I repainted my classic car in order to transform it into something so much better than it would have been, had I just allowed that rust to spread and eat away at it. From crimson to cream. And do you know what? It looks better than ever. I think Wormwood also needs to take a leap of faith on a big change that will make this town better than ever before. That is why I will be honoured if you elect me as your mayor. I have a vision for this town, and I am ready to share it with you."

He smiled and lifted his polo-shirt-clad arms just enough that it signalled the end of his speech and simultaneously encouraged applause.

"He seems like a pro," I observed.

Sean nodded. "According to Anita, he is one of the favourites for mayor. He certainly seems to have that wide appeal voters respond to. Charming, good looking… it's just a shame…"

"…that he reminds you of the old mayor?" I suggested, having had the same thought.

Sean inclined his head. "I suppose similar people have similar interests and ambitions."

"If it makes you feel any better, he's pretty gifted with magic. Not too powerful, but not too weak either," I said, hoping to differentiate between this man and the town's last mayor - who had not naturally possessed any magic at all, but had worked out a way to get around that.

A woman with shiny brown waves practically wrestled the microphone off him. A moment later, it became clear why. "My name is Lorna Carat and I am running for mayor because I believe you deserve someone better than another member of the boys' club. When my husband told me that he wanted this job, I was happy to play a supportive role. I was happy… right up until he told me that the only competition he was concerned about came from the other male candidates. That's right, ladies and gentleman… he thinks the mayor is a job for a man - regardless of their policies or aptitude for the job!" She walked across the stage, moving closer to the crowd like a speaker at a self-help conference. Her husband had been charismatic in a crisply rehearsed sort of way, but Lorna was equally compelling with her far more relatable method of speaking. "Andy always says to me: 'Honey, anything I can do I swear you can do a hundred times better!' when I've cleaned the house, or organised a social engagement. And yet, for some reason, he thinks scrubbing and garden parties are all a wife is good for! Is that the kind of man you want as mayor of this town?"

Half the room murmured their agreement that they did not want this archaic man to be in local office, or in any office at all.

"I'm not sexist!" Andy called out from the back of the stage where he was standing, waiting for other candidates to speak and join him. "This is pure fiction."

"Is this a new kind of marriage counselling? If it is, I don't like it," Sean said, baffled by what was going on.

"I take it back about Andy being hard to beat. She might dent his campaign."

"Or he'll dent hers," Sean countered, looking around at the room. A lot of women were up on their feet applauding.

"As your mayor, I won't be making any old changes I feel like, just because I can. Instead, I will constantly commune with you, the residents of this wonderful town, via social media, email, and in person. Only one person gets to be the Mayor of Wormwood, but that doesn't have to mean only one person gets to decide the future of this town."

As more applause tore through the hall, Andy Carat's mirror-practiced smile slipped and he muttered something that his wife must have overheard.

The next candidate had to coax Lorna to give up the microphone when it looked like she might be considering using it to brain her husband and get him out of the running that way. The stand-in mayor should have been the one to take charge of the situation, but she remained by the side of the stage, wringing her hands anxiously.

"Hello, I'm Jade Rey. I've lived here for the past ten years and a lot of you know me as the local history fanatic. My hobby has brought me into contact with enough of you that I now know all of your dirty little secrets and you should vote for me if you want me to stay quiet." The woman on stage - with a blonde bob that spiked out at the ends, where it was tinted bright pink - paused and pointed a finger around the entire room. There was a beat of horrified silence, before she grinned and people laughed in relief.

"A comedian, great," Sean muttered, shaking his head and looking like this was already becoming more of a mess than his worst case scenario.

"She doesn't have an ounce of magic," I informed Sean, wondering how that would bias her view of the town's history. I'd be interested to hear her take on all of the local lore and legends that she must be well versed in.

Legends... like leaving silver coins on the Devil's Jumps.

"I really think I would be a good choice for mayor because I understand how quirkiness can be a strength, and this place has got to be one of the quirkiest in the country. Thank you!" An encouraging round of applause followed.

The next candidate to approach the podium introduced herself as Rhiannon Garda. She had dark brown hair that fell in a straight sheet to just below her shoulders and wore the sort of power-suit that had first become popular in the nineties. It might be making a comeback now, but Rhiannon Garda didn't strike me as someone who felt particularly comfortable in her current attire. "She has some magic, but I doubt it's much," I said to Sean, noting the light green haze that hovered around her.

"It's not particularly cool to talk about the environment," she began, shooting the room a sad smile. "No one wants to hear about why plastic is the devil, and why using a straw that doesn't dissolve to mush in your glass of Coke should be punishable by law. Whilst I am here to offer Wormwood an opportunity to become a cleaner, greener town, I think there's a less preachy way to achieve all of this, and it comes with the side effect of making our town more beautiful. If you vote for me as mayor, I promise that there will be more green spaces, more trees planted, more protection and maintenance of our stunning forest, and community gardens everywhere for everyone to enjoy." She hesitated, momentarily searching for the next line in her speech. "Unlike many of your excellent other candidates, I don't have any kind of political background. My older brother was great at that sort of stuff. He was the favourite to become our school's student council president. When I ran for president back in my school days, I didn't win." She smiled to show that she wasn't here asking for sympathy. "What I'm trying to say is that I may not be the smoothest talker here, or have the trendiest policies, but I would do my best to deliver on my promises, and together, we can clean up Wormwood!"

Polite applause followed Rhiannon Garda's speech. She was right about people being fatigued by the same old environmental decrees, but I rather liked her idea of community gardens, more trees, and care for the forest. A lot of people took things like that for granted, but I didn't.

"Thank you, Miss *Greenpeace*," the next candidate said,

only just stopping short of an eye roll. This man sported square, wire-rimmed glasses, thinning grey hair that he'd used gel to persuade to stand on end, and a checked shirt - whose buttons were definitely under pressure to keep it together around his stomach. "I'm Graham Jinx and I have lived in Wormwood for the last twenty years. In that time, I have seen what was once a great town go to the dogs, and it's all our fault."

The audience raised its eyebrows. Had this candidate just come here to berate them?

"We need to take more pride in our town! For too long, good old fashioned values have been tossed out in favour of the passing fancies of tourism. The local youths vandalise property and litter, and the rest of us stand by and do nothing. With me as your mayor, this town will get a complete overhaul and be much better for it. I'm not talking about planting a few namby-pamby trees… what I want is neighbourhood patrols, more community events, and restoring the collective spirit and responsibility of the past that used to hold this town together. If we can unite once more, I guarantee that you will see a dramatic social change that will bring back safe Wormwood, tidy Wormwood, proud Wormwood. Vote for me and I will not let you down!"

The most half-hearted applause yet answered his call to action. I privately thought that the audience was still sulking about being blamed for the supposed decline of Wormwood. "He has some magic," I said to Sean.

He nodded, but I noticed his gaze didn't stray from the stage. His hands were tightly clenched, and I knew that we'd already reached the moment he'd been dreading. When the stand-in mayor nodded in his direction, he rose, straightening his tie as he did so.

A muttering broke out when people noticed Sean

making his way towards the front of the hall. The name that had just appeared on the projector screen hanging behind the stage belonged to a man who was no longer drawing breath.

"It is with great regret that I must inform you that mayoral candidate, Ed Brindle, has been murdered. He was found last night in Wormwood Forest and is thought to have died from deliberate decapitation."

There was a long silence as people tried to work out if this was a political stunt. The muttering increased in volume.

"Our investigation is still ongoing, and because of that, certain details must remain confidential. However, we believe that it is in everyone's interest to be aware that this crime might have had a political motive. If anyone knows of any reason why someone may have targeted Ed Brindle, or if anyone here today has felt personally threatened, please speak to me or one of my officers. There will be an almost constant police presence in Wormwood while we investigate further and follow up our current leads."

Leads they don't have, I silently thought, but I knew that Sean was trying to appear confident that the case would be solved quickly. He'd hoped that the killer would let his, or her, guard down prior to his announcement, but now he was hoping to shock them and make them think that they'd already made a mistake, which might force them to make an actual mistake.

I scanned the row of candidates, but all of them looked shocked. It was impossible to know if one of them was shocked for a different reason to the rest.

It had been a good plan… but the killer was already one step ahead of us.

The projector screen behind the candidates changed slides.

Don't lose your head like Ed, follow these rules instead!

A feeling like icy fingers rolled up my spine. This was definitely not part of the event's approved schedule.

The next slide flashed up.

Everyone here has a past they would like to hide.

Everyone has secrets.

Reveal a past regret that you have stayed silent about. Share it before midnight tomorrow by posting it as a public comment on the town hall's Mayoral Election Announcement blog post. Hang dirty laundry outside your house when you have completed this task.

No half measures. No lies. No false attempts at sincerity.

I want to know the worst thing you've ever done.

"Is this some kind of joke?" Lorna Carat said, staring at the projection screen with a mixture of confusion and concern.

The next slide took all notion of humour out of the equation.

Fail to fulfil the requirements and you will share Ed Brindle's fate.

Ed thought he could cheat his way into winning an election.

Ed got what was coming to him.

Don't be like Ed.

There was a brief pause and then the words vanished from the screen.

But the threat very definitely remained.

5

CLEARING THE AIR

"I certainly won't answer to terrorists!" Graham Jinx shouted, breaking the stunned silence that had fallen over the entire room in the wake of the startling slide show.

"Oh, I don't know. Having our secrets out in the open might not be such a bad thing," Jade Rey, the hobby historian said, looking a little smug at what she must believe was a personal absence of any political career destroying past misdeeds. "It's actually rather hard for me to think of anything truly terrible. How about you?" she asked, directing the question back at Graham, who immediately quietened down and looked furious. I privately thought that he needed to work on his debating skills, or he'd be out in the first hustings.

I looked towards Sean, who was still standing up on the stage. He was attempting to instruct Anita Heron to take control of the event, whilst also pointing his officers to investigate the source of the slideshow and figure out what was going on. In the end, Sean got his way. A very flustered Anita went back towards the podium, pausing to pick up the large, wooden box with a slot in the top of it that had been sitting on the side of the stage during proceedings. She placed it down at the front of the stage and returned to the microphone.

"Well, I think we have heard from all of the candidates present today. They will now formally submit their names and running fees into the official mayoral candidate box. If there are any yet to be declared candidates who would also like to run, now is the time to submit your name and payment," she finished with a wobbly attempt at a smile.

"Not on your life!" someone shouted out.

Anita turned pink and her hands flapped around her face, as she struggled with the unprecedented situation. "I, um…"

With a loud bang, two confetti cannons exploded. The entire room was showered with gold and silver foil pieces. In the midst of the onslaught, Jesse strode into the hall with his hands outstretched, like a famous fighter walking into the ring. "The best has been saved until last!" he announced - like he was in charge of his own commentary, too. "I, Jesse Heathen, will be entering the mayoral race. Wormwood deserves a mayor with a flair for giving people the best things in life. I am the mayor who will make your wildest dreams come true!" He pointed around the room, smiling and winking for all he was worth. I knew he was adding some devilish glamour to his words to make himself even more persuasive and likeable. I kind of hoped that the anti-cheating killer knew it, too.

Sean arrived next to me, having communed with the officers who'd been searching the building for any traces of the slideshow maker and probable killer. "Didn't he hear the ultimatum? He must have more past regrets and terrible deeds to his name than the entire population of

Wormwood combined, and he never comes across as sincere or sorry for anything."

More confetti cannons were launched courtesy of Hemlock and Hedge, signifying the end of Jesse's candidacy announcement. Amidst the confusion, Hemlock dashed over to the wooden box and dropped in the envelope that contained Jesse's fee and declaration that he was running for mayor.

"I think he might have missed that part whilst he was preparing his dramatic entrance," I commented.

"At least we now have a prime candidate for the next victim," Sean said, not looking too unhappy about that prospect.

"I wonder if he really did miss the slideshow?" I wondered out loud.

"Do we have to tell him?" Sean replied.

Anita tried to make some closing remarks and wish the candidates well in a speech that had very obviously been penned prior to any surprise slideshows. When she'd finished, she trailed off into a grateful silence and the audience just as gratefully applauded her for ending the event.

"All candidates meet backstage with me immediately. No one leaves," Sean barked when the mayoral hopefuls began milling around with the people who'd come to witness their journey into small town politics - but had instead found themselves cast as extras at the start of a scary film.

I took the opportunity to grab Jesse right as he was laughing toothily at a group of young female voters. "Did you see the slideshow that threatened death to any candidate who doesn't spill their deepest, darkest secret regret?" I asked, exasperated by his absence of alarm or prudence. "Did you make the slideshow?" I threw in for good luck.

"Do I look like the arts and crafts type to you?" Jesse

replied, reluctantly waving his female admirers away. "I did see a bit of the slideshow - enough to get the gist of it, anyway. It detracted from my own astonishing entrance into the mayoral race, which was a shame, but I think I pulled it off anyway.

"Are you really going to publicly share something you truly regret?" I asked, not believing it for a second.

Jesse shrugged. "Why not? I don't keep secrets. I'm an open book." He looked sideways at me and saw my disbelieving expression. "I suppose if I can't even convince you of that, I'd better come up with something more compelling for our killer at large." He stroked his chin. "They knew that Ed was attempting to cheat in this election. That means they probably know what it is that I do. I should come clean about that very publicly and say that I deeply regret it. That would do it, wouldn't it?"

"It might be enough to sink your campaign," I observed, brightening at the thought.

Jesse laughed, low and dark. "I doubt it. Most of the town already knows about my old profession, because they were making deals with me back when I was still in the game. Those who don't know about things like devil deals and the consequences that come attached to them will just think I'm eccentric. Consequences… that I sincerely regret." He glanced at me again. I kept my expression blank and he shrugged, apparently giving up on trying to change my opinion. "You'd be surprised by how many people are drawn to the dark side. Probably the only thing anyone could do to come out of this looking cooler than me would be to confess to the murder as their 'past regret'."

"Do you think that's something they might do?" I asked, just to see where he was going with this.

"Not a chance. Its hypocrisy, isn't it? Everyone must share their sins apart from the killer, because they are the hand of justice, not the sinner. That, and I doubt they regret murdering Ed Brindle at all," he added with a far too delighted grin.

I considered Jesse's words and realised he might have actually said something sensible for once. I was about to ask him if he had any other insights into the psychology of the murderer when Sean shouted that he would not be repeating himself again and that all candidates *meant* all candidates.

Feeling sheepish, I filed backstage with Jesse and his cat co-conspirators. Hemlock looked up at me expectantly, apparently waiting for an anticipated telling off, but by Hemlock's usual standards, it hardly even qualified as causing trouble. "Did you have fun?" I asked him instead.

"Almost," he replied. "I wanted to point my cannon at this fancy purple hat some old dear was wearing. It had plastic cherries and a fake bird on top. Hedge said that shooting it off her head would take attention away from Jesse, so I had to just follow the plan."

"You actually did what someone told you to?" I marvelled, thinking I might need to find a way to sub-contract Hedge to control Hemlock for me.

"No, I did it as a favour that he is going to repay me for." He trotted deeper into the backstage room with his tail pointed in the air. I sighed. Of course he hadn't behaved himself willingly. Sometimes, I wondered if I should take some time to attempt to teach Hemlock about the benefits of being nice and thinking of others, but some causes were about as lost as the city of Atlantis.

I followed him inside and was met with a room full of people arguing. A discussion about the identity of the person persecuting the candidates had inevitably erupted. At least a few of them were smart enough to have started wondering if it was one of their fellow hopefuls who was behind everything - trying to eliminate the competition. Fingers were being pointed in all directions and only one person looked like he was thoroughly enjoying himself.

"I bet *he* had something to do with it! He makes strange deals with people, you know," Graham said, jabbing a finger towards Jesse's smiling face.

"And how would you know that?" Andy asked the man doing the accusing.

"It's common knowledge!" Graham spluttered, but his ears were already turning red.

"Oh dear, oh dear. If I'd imagined this would happen, I'd never have called the election! I thought it was a good time to do it. So long has passed since…" Anita Heron frowned as her brain struggled to supply her with a good way to finish that sentence.

"Do you think the ultimatum applies to you, too?" Jesse asked, sidling over to the harried looking woman. "You're not technically a candidate, but it sounds like you might not want to relinquish your grip on power."

"I would never! This is just… duty!" Anita said, flustered and flapping all over again.

I marched over to Jesse and fixed him with a glare from our curiously matching eyes. "Stop stirring up trouble."

"But it's so much fun and so easy," he replied with a grin.

Fortunately, it was at that moment that Sean's police officers finished reporting back that the slideshow saboteur had left no trace of their presence behind.

Anita Heron had picked up the wooden box containing all of the candidate names and fees when Sean had demanded that everyone reconvened backstage. Now, he indicated that she should open it and lay the contents out on a handy classroom table.

"I'm sure you all must be aware of the severity of the

threat that has been placed upon everyone here today by a person, or persons, unknown. After witnessing what happened to Ed Brindle, I believe it would be prudent to take this person's threats at face value." He raised his hand when people immediately began yelling about wanting police protection and making threats of their own."Witchwood's police force will be investigating this case with all of our resources, but it is impossible to completely guarantee your safety. I would advise everyone to act with great care, and if anyone thinks they might know something about the person behind both the murder and this new threat, or if the guilty party wishes to turn themselves in, please come forward. I'm going to leave a business card with my personal phone number written on it with each and every one of you. Contact me at any time," Sean said, walking around the room and handing out his business cards.

The DCI turned back to Anita Heron, who was listlessly leafing through the names and payment envelopes. "Is there anyone who's running for mayor who isn't currently in this room?"

"Well… let's see," the ever flustered Anita said, flipping back through everything and actually reading the names this time around. "Ed Brindle hasn't submitted anything, but that's because…" she cleared her throat and shook her head, realising she was talking nonsense. "Oh! Someone from the Salem family is running, too." She lifted her head and looked at me, pushing her glasses back onto the bridge of her nose. "Is your extended family back in town?"

I strode over and grabbed the slip of paper from her hand, glancing at the name. It looked like it had been written by someone who'd used two hands to support a pen that had been too large for them to use. Or rather… two paws. "It's just a silly joke," I started to say, just as Anita opened the envelope she'd kept when I'd taken the paper from her. A fistful of cash dropped to the floor.

"I thought we were supposed to write cheques?" Rhiannon muttered, looking baffled.

"And why are they all fives? Who would pay two-hundred pounds in five-pound-notes?" Graham added.

Someone who used a spell to make a bunch of fake money, I thought, but I kept it to myself. After all, how would I come across if I confessed that my familiar had decided to run for mayor without telling me and had fabricated money, in order to trick his way into getting a place at the table?

"There was never any specific rule about cash versus cheques," Anita said, flicking through the thick wad.

"Why is she even here?" Lorna asked, crossing her arms and glaring pointedly at me.

"Hazel Salem is here representing the local press. She will be publishing official press releases relating to this case," Sean said before I could supply a reason of my own.

I did my best to not show any surprise, but I quickly realised that Sean was probably using my status as a local journalist to draw attention away from the work I did consulting for the police. I wondered if it was for my own protection, knowing that we were potentially in the company of the killer, or if there was another reason why Sean was not referring openly to my usual role.

Jesse opened his mouth to say something that would undoubtedly cause another argument, but I shot him a look so fierce that he held his tongue. I threw in a glare at Hemlock for good measure, hoping that the money wouldn't turn back into business cards until long after it had been stashed in a drawer somewhere. It was surely only because everyone was currently distracted by the events of last night and this morning that no one seemed to have noticed the suspicious aura of magic around the money. I'd thought that Jesse was the one who should be worried about incurring the killer's wrath, but there may be an even better candidate for someone with dark deeds in his past. I could only hope that when the truth about Hemlock's feline identity got out, he would be seen as a joke candidate, and the murderer wouldn't waste time delving into the past of a black cat.

"I can't believe we're standing around here like a bunch of lemons when someone has threatened to kill us, if we don't acquiesce with their incredibly unreasonable request!" Graham spoke up when the room dissolved back into muttering groups. "The police should have this under control. Who are your suspects? Who is most at risk from this mad man?"

Sean got thin-lipped over his first question, and when the second followed it, all of the eyes in the room seemed to move inexorably towards Jesse Heathen.

"I would love to see them try it," he said with a smile that hinted of danger.

All gazes immediately turned away from Jesse and pretended to focus on other things.

I frowned, knowing that it would not be an easy task to go up against someone - *something* - like Jesse. If the killer had known the nature of Ed Brindle's business with the devil, it stood to reason that they knew a thing or two about the man behind the deal. The question was, were they arrogant enough to try to make an example of him anyway? I didn't know the answer to that, but it was something worth talking to Jesse about. Somehow, I didn't think it would be too hard to convince him to break some more rules.

"Whilst I have you all here, where were each of you last

night between the hours of 11pm and midnight?" Sean asked, getting the investigation back on track.

"I was home alone," Graham said, shooting barbed glances all around, daring anyone to challenge his not exactly brilliant alibi. "Probably making a snack at that time, but no one saw me."

"I was on my own, too," Rhiannon Garda chimed in. "I watched a gardening show and then went to bed at around eleven."

"I was on my own in my workshop," Jade Rey said, shrugging her shoulders. "Working late, but I don't have anyone to back me up on that."

"I was in Wormwood Forest," Jesse said with a huge grin.

Everyone looked shocked and stared at him - except for Sean, who just looked annoyed. "Your whereabouts have already been noted, as well as your reason for being there."

"Why was he there?" Rhiannon asked - her eyes wide with a mixture of worry and curiosity.

"I'm afraid I can't tell you that," Jesse answered, as smug as a cat sunbathing on a lilo floating in a bucket full of cream.

"Because he's the killer," Graham brilliantly deduced.

"Because he has been advised by the police to not divulge details that might affect the investigation," Sean corrected, very close to losing his temper. "However, that does not exempt him, or anyone else, from being a possible suspect. Now, if you don't mind... Mr Carat, where were you?"

Everyone looked between Andy and Lorna, expecting them to be the only people with a solid alibi.

"Uh, I was in my office all night," Andy said, looking remarkably awkward.

"I was in my office... which is on the other side of the house," Lorna shared.

"Let me guess... neither of you actually saw each other?" Sean asked, doomed to accepting that his alibi exclusion idea was a complete failure.

They nodded sheepishly.

"It's like an angel of justice, isn't it?" Andy said out of the blue, rubbing his handsome chin and looking thoughtful in a carefully curated mayoral sort of way. "This person wants to make sure that the truth is told and the voters get to see the real people running for mayor - not the facades we've dreamt up. It's rather poetic really."

"Tell that to the man missing a head," Jesse sniped and set the alarmed muttering off again.

"The police should be doing more!" Graham argued.

"I think they should start by grilling all of the men in here. It would be just like a *man* to kill another *man*, because they thought he was their more serious competition," Lorna hissed.

"It would be just like a *woman* to pick the men off one by one, so they're easier to get rid of," Andy replied, shooting her a venomous look.

"Are those two really married?" Jesse asked me in a carrying stage whisper.

"Fire!" someone yelled.

"What sort of cigarette is that? I can hardly see," said another.

"Bomb!" yelled someone else.

"What on earth is happening?" - That was Sean. I recognised his voice. I couldn't see his face, as there was rather a lot of smoke in-between us.

"It's white sage!" I called out. I'd recognise the smell anywhere. Some customers seemed to expect to walk into a cloud of the stuff when they entered the apothecary.

Personally, I wasn't a fan of living in a permanent smog of incense, but I'd learned which customers liked it and had taken to telling them that the old one had burned out, and I was just putting on a new one, whenever they walked in and inevitably found me hurriedly holding a match to some dried leaves.

"Negativity out!" Rhiannon Garda shouted, drifting past me waving a baton of smoking leaves. "There's too much negativity in here! We must cleanse the room!" She vanished back into the haze.

Anita Heron did some loud throat clearing that sounded like she'd swallowed too much smoke. "Can the person burning something please put it out? You'll set off the…"

Right on cue, the fire alarm blared, deafeningly loud - which was presumably an extra measure to get the students who usually inhabited these rooms and corridors to get a move on, should there ever be an actual fire.

The room dutifully emptied of people (and cats) until Sean and I were left standing alone in the grey haze.

The DCI sighed. "I suppose that's one way to end an interview."

"I assume our Bread Cauldron Bakery date is off?" I said, glancing hopefully at him, but we both knew there would be no more dates until the mystery had been solved.

A timed task had been set by the killer. Unless we discovered who was behind the threat, the deadline could prove deadly.

6

SNEAKS AND SECRETS

I was in the Salem Apothecary the next day, thinking about the murderer's deadline, when I walked into a large piece of cardboard. It had been placed down one of the aisles, completely blocking the entrance. I backed up and realised that this particular piece of cardboard had something printed on it. Or rather, *someone*.

Hemlock's green eyes stared back at me, unnervingly at eye level. His body was several times larger than its usual size. Somehow, he'd super-imposed a golden top hat and a matching rosette onto the image. The top hat proclaimed: 'Hemlock 4 Mayor'. I stood for several moments, blinking at the cardboard cutout. Hemlock was taking this a lot more seriously than I'd given him credit for - which meant I needed to take my job of monitoring, and potentially sabotaging, just as seriously.

Because Hemlock could not become mayor.

Not unless Wormwood wanted the previous mayor's attempt at world domination and town-wide destruction to look like a teddy bears' picnic.

I shoved the cutout to the side. Many pairs of eyes

turned my way. "Am I interrupting something?" I asked my familiar.

"Yes, go away," Hemlock replied, not paying any attention to the warning in my tone of voice. He was sitting on an upturned box that had previously contained tea displayed in an artful manner to entice customers. The tea was now strewn all over the floor.

He groaned when he realised I wasn't going away. "I can run for mayor if I want! There's no age, or species, limit! Now, if you don't mind, I am having an equally legal meeting with my supporters about how we are going to take over this town and elect a familiar to rule over all who live here. Familiars first!"

"Familiars first!" the menagerie of animals cried back. Or at least, I assumed that was probably what they'd said by the loud chorus of meows, woofs, squeaks, and chirps that closely followed his final cry. Hemlock was the only animal present I could actually understand - as much as I regularly wished that was not the case.

"Run along..." my cat said, making a patronising shooing motion with his paw.

For once, I couldn't think of a good reason why he shouldn't be doing what he was doing. He'd entered using fake money that would probably come back to haunt the human with the surname 'Salem' in the near future, but aside from that bad beginning, I couldn't see why Hemlock should, or could, be banned from being a candidate, just because he was a cat and had an alarming penchant for evil deeds. "Are you going to do this fairly? You're not going to try to cheat in some way?" I enquired, figuring asking him to tell me the truth was worth a shot.

Hemlock bristled. "How dare you besmirch my honourable aims! All I want is to give the forgotten familiars a voice in this town, and we are going to achieve it any way we can!"

I bit my lip. That didn't exactly sound like he'd ruled out cheating. At some point, I would have to suggest to someone in authority that the final ballots should be checked for animal interference.

I left Hemlock to his political pandering and returned to the kitchen for a cup of tea, bumping into Aunt Linda on her way down the stairs.

"Good morning, Hazel! Any news on the maniac loose in town? Did anything happen at the candidate announcement event yesterday?" she asked, trotting over to the kettle and turning it on. Aunt Linda had been conspicuous by her absence when I'd returned from the disastrous declaration the previous day, and I thought I could hazard a guess as to why.

"No new leads on the maniac, but a lot of unexpected things happened… including a certain cat adding his name to the list of mayoral candidates and miraculously paying the fee using five-pound notes," I said, watching Aunt Linda's back stiffen when I said the last part.

She spun around with a smile on her face that was supposed to placate me. "What you saw yesterday was just an educational experiment! I never meant for the money to be used in that manner. I just wanted to see if it was possible, that was all." Her eyes drifted towards the kitchen table and then snapped back to me instantly.

I crossed my arms. "In case you're wondering, I *have* noticed the ostentatious handbag you've left on the kitchen table.

Aunt Linda coughed and turned back around to deal with the kettle. "That has nothing to do with that spell, although, I suppose I *may* have got a little mixed up with the notes in my purse. I never thought Hemlock would use his cut to enter the mayoral race. That's terrible!"

"Yes, it is," I agreed, ready to get back to Linda's part in all of this and her unethical use of fake funds.

"I can't believe he tried to use that money in front of people who can *see and use* magic. Those notes were more suspicious than a mystery meat sausage! At least I went out of town and found a large store where no one in snitching distance had even a spark of magic," Linda continued, apparently on a completely different wavelength to me.

I opened my mouth to put her straight about a few things but ended up pinching the bridge of my nose when a headache began there. "Sometimes, I think Hemlock was assigned to the wrong Salem," I commented dryly.

"He should be so lucky!" Aunt Linda said, flouncing over to the kitchen table and lovingly stroking her new bag. "Customer!" she pointed out when the bell above the shop door rang out. It had briefly been a musical bell, but the ambiguous meanings of the songs had started to drive me crazy after a while. I'd known it was time for it to go when a well-insulated man had walked in and the bell had played…

Well, it didn't matter exactly *which* song it had chosen, but it had been the wrong one.

"Good morning, careful how you go down aisle two," I said as I walked out of the kitchen area and into the shop. I was surprised to discover that I was talking to one of the mayoral candidates.

"Good morning… Hazel, isn't it?" Lorna Carat said, pushing an envelope-shaped handbag further up her forearm. She looked practically presidential today in a matching two-piece tweed jacket and skirt combination.

I managed to keep my customer-welcoming smile on my face, even though I suspected I was unlikely to make much of a profit from this exchange. "Yes, what can I do for you, Mrs Carat?"

"Ms," she corrected. I bit my tongue. I should have guessed that one. "And call me Lorna. Did I hear correctly that you're in charge of all press relating to the ongoing police investigation of the recent murder and the mayoral campaign?" she asked, pretending to examine a box of tea.

"That's right," I replied as neutrally as possible.

"Then you must already have the inside info on all of the people in the running for the big job," she said, giving up the pretence of being interested in the tea and leaning her elbows on the front desk. She rested her head in a hand and tilted it at me, like we were two best friends having a cosy chat.

"Not really. I just help to write the publicly released police statements and run the local interest magazine," I said, sensing that this woman was after more than just a positive press release. "I'll be printing something official about each and every candidate very soon. Everyone will have a chance to have their say."

"The way I heard it, you're quite friendly with the newest candidate running for mayor."

I raised my eyebrows, wondering how she'd found out Hemlock's identity.

"You know… the one with all of the charm of a devil," she added and I realised she was talking about Jesse. "I was wondering if you might be able to put in a good word for me? Perhaps we could team up for a while to boost our profiles. Beating Andy is going to be hard. He's used to coming out on top. He works as a consultant for a very successful information technology company, and hardly anyone ever says no to him. Perhaps a political alliance could give me the edge."

"Why would you pick Jesse out of all of the other candidates?" I couldn't help blurting out, knowing full well that he was almost certain to double-cross anyone who tried to work with him. Jesse also liked to make sure he never lost, and he definitely didn't care how many eggs he had to break along the way in order to do it.

"Who else am I going to pick?" she said with an abrupt laugh. "My stupid, charismatic husband needs no help to get people to like him, but I… sometimes struggle with that when I'm off the stage and back to living in the real world." She said it like it was some deep, dark secret. "The environmental one is boring. I heard that the history buff spends all of her time making weapons. Graham is both a bore and boorish, and I have no idea who that Hemlock person even is. I did ask around, thinking that if he was from your family, he might be worth my time, but no one has heard of him. That left me with Mr Heathen. I know of his reputation, of course, but you must admit, he does have a certain something about him."

"It must have passed me by," I said, possibly a little too brusquely. "I wish you luck with him," I added, trying to sound more neutral.

"I doubt I'll need luck. I can be very convincing when I want to be, and I've got the vision to win this thing. Besides… neither I, nor Andy, can afford to say no to another paying job right now, so one of us had better win it." She frowned, but didn't elaborate further on this strange tangent she'd suddenly taken.

"Why are you running against your husband?" I asked, having been curious about the answer to that question since the moment the couple had given their initial speeches.

"It's how our marriage survives!" Lorna replied, looking astonished that I may have been implying they were in dire straits. "We're very competitive. It's what drew us together in the first place. This is just another contest to us. Sometimes he wins, sometimes I do. Outside of these contests we engage in, we're as happy as can be. Happier than most of the other couples we're friends with, actually." She primped her shiny brown waves and stood upright, straightening her jacket. "Anyway, I must be on my way to chat to Mr Heathen. And I will want to see anything you've written about me before you print it, not afterwards!" she added with a pointed finger jab in my direction.

"Are you worried about the deadline?" I asked just as she was pulling the door open to leave. It was another thing I was desperately, and perhaps morbidly, curious about.

"Sharing a secret past regret? Not at all. I have a ton of regrets. My therapist encourages me to talk about them openly. This is almost like free therapy." And with that final announcement, she left the shop that I knew she'd only entered to see if she could worm her way into Jesse's good graces.

"I wonder what gave her the idea that I was in his good graces, and he in mine?" I muttered, thinking dark thoughts about Jesse Heathen and all that he'd done in the past. We were supposed to have called it quits, but he certainly had a way of bringing up ancient history.

I was still thinking dark thoughts directed at just about everyone I'd encountered so far this morning when the shop door opened again and a second person involved in the mayoral election entered.

"Good morning, I would like to buy some herbs," stand-in mayor, Anita Heron said, walking up to the counter with the sort of forced buoyancy I recognised as someone who has psyched themselves up prior to an encounter.

"Do you really want to buy some herbs?" I asked before

I could stop myself, exceedingly skeptical after my last visitor.

"Why else would I be here? This is an apothecary, isn't it?" Anita asked, showing some spunk, before doubt crept in at the end of her sentence and rather ruined it.

I managed an apologetic smile realising that I was the one in the wrong for having judged her too soon. "You wouldn't know it by the morning I've had so far," I explained. "What can I do for you?"

"Cayenne pepper, dried lemon slices, black peppercorns, rue, and… some white sage," she added with a shrug. "Maybe Rhiannon has the right idea about the air needing to be cleared. It doesn't hurt to try, does it?"

"Of course not," I agreed with a smile, back to being a shop owner, who believed the customer was always right.

"That, and it does seem to offer a hasty end to arguments when they arise," she added more cynically. "Oh! Goodness me!" Anita had turned around and discovered the huge cutout of Hemlock. She put a nervous hand on her heart and read the words written on the hat the giant cat was wearing. "So *that's* Hemlock Salem! Is this why you were so mysterious about that late entry yesterday? You entered your cat as a protest candidate?" She tilted her head and carried on talking whilst my brain was still trying to formulate a response to her incorrect assumption."He looks very sweet in that outfit. You must have such a lovely close bond! With all of the controversy surrounding the election, I wouldn't be surprised if some people voted for your cat in protest. A cute fuzzy cat in an outfit could be just what Wormwood needs."

"He's far from cute and fuzzy. He's actually…" I tried to say, but Anita wasn't listening.

"I think what amazes me most is that no one has dropped out after those horrible words came up on screen.

If it was me running for mayor, I'd have been out of there faster than you could say 'uh-oh spaghetti-O'. I suppose they must all be very serious about the welfare of Wormwood."

"Something like that," I said, thinking about Jesse and Hemlock when I said it.

"I know most of the candidates pretty well, you know," Anita said, far more chatty than she'd been behind the microphone. "I went to secondary school with Lorna, Andy, Rhiannon, and Jade. I was in Andy's year, while the others were all a couple of years younger than me. Not many years younger," she added, patting down her hair and semi-hoping for a compliment. "It wasn't the happiest school experience ever. There were so many tragedies. Rhiannon's older brother died in a car accident. He was in the same school year as me, so you can imagine how shaken up we all were! You never think about things like death when you're that age. Then, poor Andy's dad died in a helicopter accident. Oh, and Lorna's guinea pig passed away and she managed to be excused from more classes than you would *believe* on compassionate grounds." She rolled her eyes. "I remember her making a bigger deal out of it than Andy, who had a real tragedy in his life."

"That's awful," I said, wondering why she was painting Andy's misfortune as more personally tragic than anyone else's. Death was a terrible thing for secondary school-aged teenagers to have to deal with.

"Andy's dad wasn't even in the helicopter at the time. It fell out of the sky and hit him when he was popping to the shops to buy milk. Andy was devastated." She sighed and her eyes grew misty with sudden emotion. "I think that's why he's so committed to returning to politics. It's what his dad would have wanted. He'll be a good mayor if he wins."

I inwardly arched my eyebrows at Anita's lack of impartiality. "They're all impressive candidates," I said, doing my bit to stay neutral. I was fortunate that the killer didn't seem to be judging anyone outside of the election for telling lies.

"Yes, yes… of course," Anita agreed halfheartedly, counting her money onto the front desk. "Thank you for the herbs," she added, popping the bag into her pocket and returning to the sunny street outside.

"How DARE she?" a feline voice screeched the second the door swung shut.

I peered over the top of the cardboard cutout at the very offended black cat standing behind it. His fellow familiars seemed to have already left to spread the word. "How dare she call you cute and fuzzy?"

"No! I mean, yes, that too, but no! How dare she call me a protest vote. I'll show her. I'll show all of you!" he said, turning and stalking out of the shop towards the kitchen with his tail tall and bristling.

I bit my lip when I heard the sound of the cat flap opening and shutting behind him. Something told me that the trouble in Wormwood was only just beginning.

7

WEAPONS OF MASS PRODUCTIONS

Sean didn't arrive until the late afternoon. My mood had lifted since the morning, with both Hemlock's absence and the arrival of people who were genuinely interested in making purchases and not involved with the upcoming election. Even so, seeing Sean walk in clutching an armful of brown folders made it plummet again.

"I've brought the information that's been gathered so far on all of the candidates. We have no leads on anyone outside of the mayoral race at the moment, so the best we can do is start our search within it. Either we'll find the killer there, or we may find something that the killer already knows and is planning to use to target one of the candidates," he added, a lot less cheerfully.

"Don't you have a big team working on this?" I asked. The folders didn't exactly look inviting.

"Not big enough. We've been rushed off our feet trying to work on the Ed Brindle case and organise security for the other candidates. You live in Wormwood, so I was hoping that you might notice something that stands out, which might have been missed by others. A background check team put these together, but this is the first opportunity I've had to get them in front of someone."

"I think I might have already found something interesting out this morning. Lorna Carat came by and 'just happened' to slip into conversation that the history fan, Jade Rey, makes weapons," I said with all of the skepticism over Lorna's motivations that her declaration deserved.

"She makes weapons?" Sean repeated, raising an eyebrow and flipping through the folders until he found the right one and opened it. His second eyebrow joined the first. "Well, she did say that history was her hobby. It would appear that Jade's job is making weapons that are used in television and film. She specialises in medieval weaponry."

"So, swords and axes and other sharp things like that," I commented. "She failed to mention it during her opening speech."

We exchanged a look, both wondering if the reason why she was trying to keep her job quiet was the obvious one. Few things could be more obviously suspicious than a weapons maker just happening to be running for mayor at the same time as another candidate lost his head.

Sean glanced at the stack of folders in his hands again and then dumped the lot of them on the table I used for tea drinking, that was situated in a quiet corner of the apothecary. "Finding a suspect in five seconds. I suppose that's one way to get out of doing this reading," he observed, before the faintest of smiles appeared on his lips. "I think it's time we paid a visit to Jade Rey... let's find out if our weapons maker is planning to turn into a sword swinger at the strike of twelve."

"I didn't see a fact file on Hemlock?" I joked when we were in Sean's car on our way to the address that Jade Rey had given to the Witchwood police when they had contacted all of the candidates, after the threat against them had been made, to offer protective services.

"Most of my colleagues already think I've lost my mind, working too many cases in Wormwood. I think commissioning a background check on a cat would be the final straw."

I looked out of the window at the creeping twilight as we drove through town. The killer had given everyone a clear deadline, and we still had plenty of time.

It just went to show, you should never trust a murderer.

* * *

The evening was definitely drawing in when Sean pulled up outside Jade Rey's home. It was located on the outskirts of town in a direction I'd seldom wandered in, and even if I had, I doubted I would have noticed anything remarkable about the property. The only hint that it wasn't just an ordinary house was the handcrafted metal sign on the garden gate, which read: 'The Weapons Workshop' and featured letters forged from mangled knives and skew-whiff swords.

"This all looks completely normal," Sean muttered.

"Perhaps it's not what it looks like," I said, confidently walking up to the solid oak gate that separated the workshop area from the road outside and hammering on it. "They could all be fake - made to look real on a television screen, but not actually sharp," I suggested, reaching out and touching the edge of one of the bent swords.

I looked at the cut on my finger and reflected that touching it to check really hadn't been necessary, or smart. The gate swung open and I concealed my finger behind my back, hoping no one would notice.

"If you're worried about my safety, thanks for the offer of police security, but I've got it handled," Jade Rey said, coolly resting the broadsword she'd answered the gate holding over her shoulders.

When we said nothing, her smug expression turned to one of understanding. She looked back at the sword. "Ah. You're not here to enquire about my safety. I suppose I should have seen this coming. Would you like to come inside?"

We hesitated.

Jade propped the sword up against the inside wall. "How about now?"

We followed her into her workshop and discovered what had to be the biggest collection of weaponry in the county - possibly only surpassed by large castles in the rest of the country. Trebuchets were mounted on the walls, morning-stars dangled from the ceiling of her workshop barn, and spears were mounted in racks - apparently for easy access. Jade Rey was ready to supply an entire army for a war I'd never heard of.

"As I am sure you have already discovered, my job is to make weapons for film and television productions. I also do a few custom bits for the occasional fan of history, films, or shows who wants to own a perfectly made replica item," she said gesturing around.

I looked sideways at Sean.

"If you're wondering why I didn't mention it in my introductory speech, it's because not everyone likes the work I do here. They think it promotes violence, which is ridiculous. I deliberately didn't share my job because it doesn't represent my policies. My policies are about the preservation of history and its revival, not about waving swords around. I don't make a secret of what I do, but I didn't want it to muddy things."

Sean cleared his throat. "Did you murder Ed Brindle using one of your weapons?"

That's one way to get to the point, I thought, surprised Sean wasn't trying a more subtle approach. Then, I remembered we were standing in a room filled with weaponry. I decided that subtlety was probably not the right approach.

Jade shook her head. "No! I'm probably the least suspicious candidate *because* I'm the most suspicious. It's too obvious, isn't it? I'd have to be crazy to write ultimatums and go around beheading people when my day job is making weapons. The first place the police would come knocking would be at my door!" She looked back and forth between us. "This *is* the first place you've come knocking, isn't it?"

We shuffled our feet.

Jade sighed. "Look, I know I have the equipment and - quite frankly - the skillset to pull off some old-school style beheadings. Also, it would be quite fun to test the weapons I make in a real life situation." She cleared her throat, realising that now was probably not a good time for that confession. "But… it wasn't me! I want to win this election fair and square. Wormwood is a weird town, and I do think the locals are a bit crazy with all of their talk about magic - some of them have started to believe their own tourist tales! But, I love this town and the weird things about it. I just wanted to celebrate all of that history and encourage the entire town to be interested in their past, you know?"

"What past regret are you thinking of revealing?" I asked, hoping to catch her out. The guilty person may not have bothered to come up with anything at all. Alternatively, they could be too confident, having thought out their story well in advance, because they'd had a lot longer than twenty-four hours to consider it.

Jade shrugged and reached out for a dagger, polishing it with a rag whilst she thought it over. "I've been struggling with that, to be honest. The best I've been able to come up with was that I once deliberately put grease all over the handle of a claymore when a particularly obnoxious actor was due to film a fight scene. He'd complained the sword wasn't heavy enough, so I thought it would be funny to see him keep dropping it, after acting so tough. Unfortunately, he did drop the sword, and it chopped his toes off… which was taking the joke too far," Jade confessed. "I honestly don't have anything better than that. When I want to do something, I go right ahead and do it. I wanted to make swords and axes and stuff, so I trained to do that. I'm not the sort of person who has many regrets, as I don't let opportunities pass me by."

All in all, it was a pretty good answer.

Even though neither of us was truly expecting to find a bloodstained blade hanging up on the wall (well, not one stained with *real* blood anyway) we still searched the workshop, just to make sure. By the time the night had rolled in, we hadn't found anything that might suggest Jade was the killer.

"Don't mind me, just hanging out my dirty laundry," she said when we were standing by the gate again, wondering what - if anything - we'd learned today.

A cold fist gripped my stomach with the visual reminder that time had almost run out.

"I didn't think it would take this long," Sean murmured, looking as shellshocked as I felt. Neither of us wanted to say it, but Jade Rey had seemed so likely, so plausible, that we'd mentally placed all of our eggs of suspicion in one Jade Rey-shaped basket.

"I shared my regret to the town hall blog earlier. Hopefully, it will be enough to satisfy the mystery murderer," Jade said, sounding quite chipper about the whole thing. I surmised it was probably because, when you were surrounded by a self-made armoury, other people with sharp-edged weapons don't concern you as much as they would the average person. "Confessing what I did may affect my business, but to be honest, I've never met anyone who liked that actor. I suppose he could sue me over it - at the time, it was classed as an accident - but I'll probably get more work from those who hate his guts, which will make up for it. What will be, will be," she said with an easy shrug.

"Do you have police officers watching all of the candidates?" I asked when we'd said goodbye to Jade and were standing on the road outside her house.

"I had a few problems with that," Sean confessed. "Each and every one of the mayoral candidates - with the exception of Hemlock - was offered police security in the form of a car outside of their houses to keep an eye on things and offer a quick response, should anything happen. Unfortunately, according to one of my officers, there is now a group chat online between the candidates. They collectively decided that they didn't want any security, claiming it's akin to a confession of fear. Instead, they want to stand up to this criminal and demonstrate that they won't cower before them."

"But they're all still planning on sharing their secret past regrets, aren't they?"

Sean shot me a knowing look. "Yes, caution seems to have overcome rebellion in that aspect. In truth, I got the feeling that some of the candidates have taken a dim view of the police in the light of what happened to Ed and our failure to wrap things up neatly inside of a day." He sighed. "In any case, there are still cars parked outside of all of their houses. The only difference is, the police officers are wearing plainclothes and keeping their distance. The candidates aren't criminals - well, not *proven* criminals - so, everything is being done at a distance to respect their wishes." He nodded down the street to where a grey BMW was parked within sight of Jade Rey's red-brick house. "All of the candidates are being watched. Nothing should go wrong tonight."

Sean's phone rang in his pocket.

He pulled it out and answered, his expression immediately morphing into a frown as soon as the person on the other end of the line spoke.

"It's Andy Carat," Sean mouthed, his face growing darker with every word that was said to him.

The monologue on the other end of the line went on for what felt like an eternity. I was suddenly hyper aware of the hairs on my arms rising upwards.

"Stay where you are. We are on our way right now." Sean ended the call and shoved his phone back into his pocket, indicating that we should get into the car. He turned the key in the ignition. "He's at the library. He says there's someone in there with him."

And that was how we found ourselves abandoning the suspicious swords, daggers, and spears of Jade Rey to pursue someone who might have a completely different axe to grind.

8

CHECKING OUT

"Did he mention what he was doing in the library after closing time?" I asked as the car tore down almost empty streets, chasing across town towards a man in mortal peril.

"He claimed that he was anxious about what might be happening after midnight tonight, so he decided to pop out to the library to do some research earlier in the evening. He must have sneaked out, because I haven't received a report of movement from my officers. It was hard to hear him because he was whispering, but he seems to have heard some sort of noise that he wasn't expecting to hear whilst in the library after closing time. He thought it best to seek shelter, and he found my business card in his pocket and called for help."

"Very heroic," I said, uncharitably.

"Very sensible," Sean corrected, just as I deserved. He shook his head and his mouth set in a line as we pulled into a space outside of the library that was only illuminated by the streetlights outside the building. It had been a while since I'd visited this place. The last time had been when a mysterious librarian had arrived in town. There wasn't any specific reason why I'd avoided the library after that. It was ridiculous to think that history repeating itself could be avoided by me staying away from a place that had once been tied up with trouble, but I'd avoided it all the same.

Tonight seemed to be proof that a pointless ritual, like staying away from the library, had not been sufficient to stop anything bad from occurring inside its walls.

"Do you think he already put his dirty laundry out?" I said to Sean to smooth things over, whilst wondering about the scorn I suddenly felt for Andy Carat. He had every right to be wherever he wanted to be at any time of the day and night. It was a free country. The only reason I was wondering what a grown man was doing staying out so late in a public building was because the killer had made me want to scrutinise every single one of the candidates.

"Shouldn't we have back up?" I asked, suddenly getting a bad feeling about this. Some might say it was intuition that led me to believe there was something awful waiting inside the building we were about to enter, but even though I was no longer one to doubt things like intuition and premonition, I was also aware that it often came from signs seen and internalised without us even realising it. In this case, the sign was the front door of the library, left slightly ajar - even though it was well after closing time.

Sean pulled the door open and cautiously stepped inside the building. "The security system isn't armed. You usually need a code to stop the alarm going off. Andy let me know that the librarian told him to arm it whenever he left the library. He said that staying after hours is no big deal and he knows the door codes. Apparently, quite a lot of people in town do. If you're nice to the librarians, the librarians are nice to you."

"Letting someone use the library late at night isn't exactly the crime of the century. I'm sure many of the librarians would be happy to be handed a little bit extra on top of their regular pay. He said all of this whilst in fear for his life?" I found it strange that so much detail had been passed to Sean when Andy was claiming to be in mortal peril.

"He was probably trying to distract himself from his situation by focusing on logic. Panic makes people act unusually."

"So does having a murderous agenda against a group of political candidates," I observed pithily.

All was silent when we entered the library.

The main lights had been turned off, but there was still a reading light left on next to one of the heavily varnished tables, where patrons could sit and read books. It was towards this table and the pool of light that Sean and I moved, drawn to the comforting sign of humanity.

What we found there was quite the opposite.

He was sitting just beyond the pool of light, which was why we hadn't spotted him immediately. The chair had been pushed back, almost against the bookshelves behind the table, as if the person sitting in it had moved his chair that way in order to stand up very quickly.

He hadn't been fast enough.

I took a deep breath, hoping it would calm me down, but the smell of death was in the air - a copper tang that permeated everything. Now that we were much closer, the shadows cast by the little light seemed to make everything even more jarring than it would have been under the fluorescent tubes on the ceiling. The dark red stain on the carpet that would be beyond cleaning and have to be ripped out and replaced, the splinters of wood from the bookshelf behind the chair that had fallen to the floor, and the severed head, sitting almost nonchalantly a metre away from the body in the chair.

My breathing shallowed, before I managed to persuade it to return to normal.

When Ed Brindle had been murdered, it had occurred outside and on an ancient rock covered with vegetation, making the surface far from smooth or clean in the first place. In the midst of the forest, the first scene hadn't seemed so... so *real*. It was a strange thing to think, but that was the thought that wouldn't leave my head when I looked at this new murder. Things were so much messier when they happened inside.

The method of murder had been messier than the first, too, I finally acknowledged, forcing myself to look at the body again. Ed's head had been removed in a single, smooth swipe. This time was different... a greater number of strokes, less clean, more rushed. I wondered if the killer had made a mistake.

"It's not Andy Carat," I said out loud when the silence had stretched on for half a minute at least.

"No, it isn't," Sean agreed, sounding grateful that I'd managed to break the spell of shocked silence without focusing too minutely on what we were actually looking at. "It's Graham Jinx, isn't it?" he said, but we both knew the identity of the headless man.

I wondered about the candidate who'd met such a terrible end in the library. He'd been at that age when career success has usually peaked and some people look at their lives reflectively and say 'What more is there?' It was often referred to as a mid-life crisis, but I thought it should instead be referred to as a midlife re-evaluation - not something to be mocked or feared, but an opportunity to bring about genuine change.

Unfortunately for Graham Jinx, the most recent change

that had occurred in his life was not something that could be reversed.

"We should check what secret past regret he shared," I said, noticing that the dark green glass of the desk lamp had several darker spots on it. I glanced down at the worn carpet Sean and I were standing on and silently acknowledged that we'd probably already got too close and were standing in the middle of the crime scene.

There was a laptop on the table, which had been left slightly open - just enough so that the light didn't turn out. Sean pulled on a pair of gloves and gingerly lifted the lid, expecting to see the town hall's website appear on the screen with a comment left by Graham that hadn't cut the mustard with the murderer.

It wasn't the town hall's site that popped up, but something else entirely. An Excel spreadsheet with monetary figures written in the rows and columns. I wasn't sure what they meant, but a handy note from the killer had been added that saved me from doing the maths.

New comment from Graham Jinx: I siphoned money from the accounts of the companies I did bookkeeping for, abusing their trust for my own personal gain.

I should have regretted doing this.

I bet you regret it now.

The last line was in a different font - clearly a comment from the killer.

I pulled out my phone and logged onto the library's internet, quickly bringing up the town hall's blog. Graham had left a comment, but it wasn't the one written on the laptop screen.

"I, Graham Jinx, regret the many cruel words I said to my now ex-wife during the time that led up to our divorce. I have never told anyone this, because I viewed it as a sign of weakness to admit I was wrong. I hope that she will forgive me," I read out loud. "Someone didn't think he was being sincere. The killer thought Graham was sitting on a better secret from his past," I observed.

"Someone believes they have the right to make that judgement," Sean replied, his expression granite. "We can't stay here. There's a person in this building who's unaccounted for," he reminded me.

I shook myself and nodded. In the light of the grim discovery, I'd completely forgotten about Andy Carat. For his sake, I hoped the killer had overlooked him, too.

We turned away from the silent remains, entering the rows of shelves lined with books. I wondered if we were looking for a second victim, a survivor, or perhaps even the killer himself.

The last thought made me wonder.

According to Sean, Andy had shared a lot of information on the phone. He'd justified it as Andy latching onto something logical to quell his fear of the unknown horror that was happening beyond his hiding place... possibly even stalking him in the dark. But I wondered if the invitation to the library had come courtesy of the killer, who was now playing the victim to make himself appear above suspicion.

Sean's torch flashed around the corner of the last stack of shelves, revealing a row of computer desks with the monitors all displaying screen savers. The beam of his torch bounced off something pale and organic. Human flesh. My heart skipped for a moment, before the skin the light had caught moved, and Andy Carat unfolded himself from under the desk where he'd been hiding.

"Is it safe? Has he gone?" he asked, a tremor in his voice.

"We saw no sign of an intruder being in the building currently," Sean said, keeping his words vague.

Andy picked up on the slight hesitation that followed Sean's words. "Something's happened, hasn't it? What is it you're not telling me?"

"Mr Carat, do you know if anyone else was present in the library at the time of your call? And what was it that made you believe that there was someone else in here who posed a potentially deadly threat to you?" he asked.

Andy frowned, his handsome face looking concerned in the carefully curated manner that presidents and prime ministers like to use whenever there's a disaster they have to express condolences for. "It's probably better if I just tell you everything I remember prior to your arrival. I wouldn't want to miss any detail that you might think is important. I arrived before closing time and then I stayed late, going through some records on the computer. Jordan, the librarian, came by to say they were closing up, but I've often stayed late before. I have an office in my house where I do most of my work, but I've always liked the library. There's something about the place that encourages focus, don't you think? That, and sometimes the walls and door of my office simply aren't enough distance between me and Lorna," he admitted, a little more sheepishly. "I was researching the past mayors of Wormwood, hoping to find some inspiration. A lot of the town's archives have been converted to digital format. It was supposed to be something to amuse me and keep me from thinking too much about the threat hanging over all of our heads. I doubt I'm the only one who felt that way. I know my wife left the house via the back garden before I did, so she's probably off somewhere distracting herself, too. I posted the past regret that I've kept secret to the website, and there's dirty laundry hanging outside of my house."

He took a deep breath, knowing that he'd arrived at the important part. "About ten minutes after Jordan left, I think I heard the library door open, but I can't be sure. I do remember hearing the coffee machine whirring a while after that, but I figured it might just be automatically turning off."

"The library has a coffee machine?" Sean interjected, looking surprised.

"It's quite a trendy library these days," Andy said. "That, and the people in charge thought that free coffee and tea might bring in the younger generation and persuade them to read some actual books. They thought it was worth the risk of occasional spillages to keep the books from sitting around, gathering dust. Times change, don't they?" He cleared his throat, realising he'd been sidetracked. "I didn't really consider whether anyone else was in here. I was engrossed in my reading. The next thing I remember hearing was like a deep, hollow thunk. It happened twice more." He ran a hand through his luxuriant hair. "I just thought it sounded wrong somehow. That was when I decided to hide and call you. Half of me wanted to go and take a look, in case I'd just run like a scared rabbit from a book falling off a shelf, but I don't know… I just sensed that something wasn't right, and I decided that the risk of embarrassment was better than the risk of death."

Sean and I considered his words in silence.

"Is someone dead?" Andy asked, his throat bobbing visibly as he swallowed. He'd worked out why we were asking about a second person being in the library - one who wasn't the killer.

"Yes," Sean told him. "Another candidate. Did you hear anything after the noises you reported?"

"Uh, I think I heard the fire exit open and close. I don't know," he said, his eyes drifting inexorably back in the direction we had come from.

"You're not certain?" I said unbelievingly, silently thinking that the killer could still be inside the library after all, having changed his clothes for a clean set and slipped into the role of almost-victim.

"Where's the fire exit?" Sean asked, picking fact-finding over interrogation.

Andy gestured towards the opposite corner of the library. The back wall and exit were hidden from view by more rows of shelving. "I think it's supposed to be connected to a fire alarm, but you know how things go in public buildings… a child sets it off one time too many, and the people who work here snap and disconnect the darned thing - just so they don't lose their sanity."

Our conversation was interrupted by the sound of the library door opening.

"Identify yourself!" Sean called out. We all held our breath in the silence that followed.

"Back up?" I whispered to him, but he didn't look certain, patting his pocket in a way that made me think no one had contacted him to confirm their position yet.

"Urgh! Gross! You'd think people would take more care when they're murdering someone," a voice said from the direction of the entrance.

I knew there was only one man in Wormwood who would skip being horrified by the violence on display and instead criticise the killer for not doing a better job.

9

NO REGRETS

"Jesse, what are you doing here? This is a crime scene! Go away!" I yelled back, turning away from one suspicious candidate to go and tangle with another.

"I'm just here because I fancied taking out a book to read. The librarian gave me the door code ages ago, in case you're wondering how I got in." He let out a low whistle when I rounded the bend of the final shelves and returned to the open area where the tables were. I discovered he was standing right in front of the body, looking at the laptop screen. "Someone got caught with their hand in the company cookie jar."

"Get away from there!" Sean barked.

I turned around and realised both men had followed when I'd stalked off to deal with Jesse. Someone definitely needed to have a word with these librarians about whom they handed out codes to. Wormwood's library appeared to have become a twenty-four hour library without officially being so.

I glanced at the table again and realised that the laptop was the only thing on it. There was no sign of a coffee cup.

"Oh. Oh good grief. Is that Graham Jinx?!" Andy said, stepping out from behind Sean.

I spared him a long look, checking to see how he was reacting to what should be a traumatic sight for anyone. Or at least - for anyone who wasn't personally responsible for creating the shocking scene. And also Jesse, who had been in this world for so long that things like this bounced straight off him.

Andy's tanned face had turned pale. There was a sheen on his forehead that was undoubtedly sweat of the cold kind. It was a convincing performance, but I reminded myself that all of the people running for mayor were aspiring politicians, and politicians are not exactly renowned for their liberal use of the truth. Perhaps some of the candidates were more practiced politicians than others.

"His secret was pretty rubbish," Jesse said, sitting on a nearby table and surveying the scene. "That's why I came here. I figured that out of everything everyone shared, ol' Graham's tale of woe was the limpest lettuce of the lot."

I bit my lip, realising that Sean and I should have done the same. We'd been so sure that Jade had to be involved, and then the killer had moved the deadline forward. It was barely ten o'clock. "Did everyone post something?" I asked, wondering if I'd hit on the reason for the earlier than planned judgement.

"They certainly did," Jesse said, his mouth quirking up at one side, as he revelled in the drama.

"You came here because you knew Graham was going to be murdered? That's not suspicious *at all*," Andy commented sarcastically, regaining some colour and narrowing his eyes at yet another of his rivals.

"It *is* rather suspicious," I wholeheartedly agreed with him, raising my eyebrows at Jesse. We both knew he hadn't been the one swinging the weapon, but I didn't see why he shouldn't be made to squirm for striding in uninvited.

"What about you, Andy? Someone must have reported Graham's fate to our local law enforcement official. Does that mean you were here when this murder happened?" Jesse asked, flipping it back on the other man in an instant. Loathe as I was to admit it, Jesse was certainly cut out to be a politician.

"I had a perfectly good reason to be here, which I have explained and justified to DCI Admiral. I certainly wasn't up to no good!" Andy replied, his eyes becoming steel in an instant. "You're the one who's turned up so conveniently right after a murder has been committed. You would have had just enough time to skip home and change out of your murder outfit!"

"I'm glad you think I'm a classy enough killer to have a special outfit for committing murders in," Jesse replied, not doing himself any favours at all. A wicked smile stretched his lips. "What was that secret past regret you shared again? I did read them all, but some people have gripping lives and others don't…" he said, heavily implying that Andy Carat was as dull as dishwater.

"It was a lot more sincere and convincing than your confession!" He cleared his throat and pretended to mimic Jesse's voice. "Once, I pretended to be a bride to convince a giant to marry me, which I definitely regret, because giants are not very good looking and I feel I could have done better." He shook his head. "Is that even true?"

"Nearly," Jesse said with a shrug. "I may have had to borrow some past regrets from close family. I've already made my peace with all that I've done. Your past regret was something about not taking a business opportunity, wasn't it? You kept the offer to yourself and didn't act upon it until it was too late? It's interesting that you picked something like that. I thought your past regret might be more to do with current family financial issues caused by your past actions. That's what I heard anyway."

"I thought you didn't remember what I'd written?" Andy said, but his expression had darkened. Jesse had touched a nerve.

I wondered where he'd got that information from and decided that Lorna had caught up with him after all. Clearly, she hadn't been shy about sharing a few more secrets with a fellow candidate. I stowed the information away for later consideration. I didn't know how near to the mark Jesse was with his hints, but judging by Andy's reaction, something had hit close to home.

"I don't know how we can be standing here having a normal conversation when Graham is… is that," Andy said, his confident voice suddenly overcome with tremors. He gulped and took a good long look at what had befallen his rival, morbid curiosity getting the better of him. "That is some poor quality axe work," he said.

"Axe work?" Sean queried, immediately picking up on the certainty behind Andy's words.

The other man shot him a curious glance, but he returned his gaze to Graham and nodded his head at the bookshelf behind the headless body. "Yes, surely you can tell by the divots in the wood where the axe twisted upon impact? That, and the multiple swings it took." He gulped and stayed silent for a moment. Swallowing before continuing. "It's pretty hard to get a clean horizontal swing to go exactly where you want it to go and do the job in one. Axes work by utilising the weight of the head, which is why you chop wood by raising the axe upwards. It does half of the work for you when you bring it down. The same goes for executions back in the old days. There's a reason why they made them kneel and put their head on a block."

Jesse looked delighted. "Listen to him! He's basically confessing!"

"I'm not confessing to anything! I just have some knowledge on the topic because it's a hobby of mine. You wouldn't understand," Andy retorted, visibly furious that Jesse was rallying against him.

"Hobby?" Sean said, nowhere near as amused as Jesse was about this.

Andy puffed his chest out. "I am a competitive woodchopper - a champion, actually," he announced, like it was the most normal thing in the world.

Jesse broke the silence. "You know... that excuse is so terrible, it might just be true."

Sean put a hand to his pocket where his phone was. Two seconds later, the library door burst open.

"Police!" the first officer shouted, shining her torch into the darkened room, before spotting our little group standing close to the reading light illuminated table.

"This is a crime scene, cordon off the area," Sean barked in response, looking less than impressed that it had taken so long for his officers to make their way across town from where they'd failed to keep a close watch on their different targets. I wondered if the killer had managed to slip their own surveillance and sneak out without being spotted, too. It seemed all too plausible.

Sean directed his small posse of police officers to tape off the area, having called the forensics team to come and gather any evidence, and the coroner to eventually remove the body. Two other officers were busy collecting statements from Jesse and Andy when Sean turned to me, rubbing his eyes so roughly that they looked red when he removed his hands. I could tell my boyfriend was exhausted, but there would be no rest for him tonight after what had happened here.

"I'll walk you out," Sean said.

"I'm sure there'll be some evidence that will bring something to light," I told him, trying to find a silver lining in this disastrous night when we were back outside in the cool, early summer air.

"I hope so," Sean agreed, looking older and more tired than ever in the glow of the streetlights. "It's hard for my police force when none of them has an ounce of magical ability, to my knowledge. I think a couple of them might be shape-shifters. There are whispers that it's common in Witchwood, but it's something unspoken, and I don't think it would ever be a good idea to run around asking if anyone gets a bit furrier during the full moon."

I nodded understandingly. Some things did need to remain unsaid. There'd been a time when I'd thought that the idea of magic being real was laughable, and that most of Wormwood was well and truly off its rocker. I'd put it down to superstition and a need to keep things weird for the few tourists the town indulged, who'd heard of Wormwood's reputation. It was only when I'd witnessed strange happenings first hand and had finally been able to see magic that I'd accepted its existence. We both knew that if Sean broke ranks and started talking about magic to the people who worked for him, he'd probably be out of a job faster than you could say 'nervous breakdown'.

"Perhaps there's something that can be done about it," I mused.

"I hope you're not talking about the glasses that make magic visible, which your father made? I've still got them, but I don't think it would be a good idea to start producing them and reveal to the entire world that magic is real and visible with these trendy new glasses. It could be profitable, but…"

"Not a good idea," I finished for him with a thin smile. It was true that my inventive father had managed to work out a way for a non-magically gifted person to see the same light trails that someone using witch sight could see, but even my father hadn't injected too much enthusiasm into that particular invention. Enabling someone who already knew about magic through repeated exposure to it (like Sean) to see magic was a world away from indoctrinating someone into a brand new world they had no idea existed. There was always a temptation to take something new, share it with the world, and call it progress, but not all progress was good. Progress could also be made in the wrong direction.

"Besides, money just brings trouble," I said with another slim smile. Courtesy of my father's rather prematurely announced death and subsequent will, I didn't have to worry about money these days. It was a nice change from scraping around for enough cash to get some groceries that weren't baked beans, but I'd already cracked that prior to the inheritance. The money from the company shares I'd inherited and sold was still sitting in the bank, ready for whatever rainy day came next.

We hadn't spoken about it, but I wondered if Sean was in a similar situation. I'd visited his house when he'd had something nasty delivered to him during an investigation that had got too personal, and I'd been astonished when the castle-like building hadn't fitted with my preconceived idea of a place where Sean would spend his nonworking hours. It was a little strange that he hadn't invited me round before, or since, but we'd always spent most of our time together in Wormwood. Things had just continued that way.

Deep down, I knew there was something Sean was keeping from me, but I was also happy enough to let him take his time in sharing it. The right moment would arise, I was sure of it. I would be patient.

But it had better be sooner, rather than later.

I blinked and realised that Sean had said something and I'd missed it.

He sighed but let me off the hook, thankfully assuming that my moment of inattention was due to the horrific crime scene in the library and not to do with a mystery mansion and the DCI, who was the unlikely inhabitant. "You should go home, Hazel. I'll call if I need you. Get some rest."

"We'll solve this, don't worry," I said, wanting to support the man I had grown to love during our many adventures together.

"Sooner rather than later," Sean agreed, echoing the thought I'd just had about the man I was speaking to right now.

I nodded grimly. The killer might think of themselves as some sort of angel of justice, exposing the lies of the people who wanted to lead the town, but no one had the right to take a life away from another person. And when it came to keeping past misdeeds a secret, this killer was as big a hypocrite as they came.

10

MYSTERIOUS CIRCUMSTANCES

The Salem Apothecary's shop window had vanished completely when I arrived back home from the library. Someone had plastered so many posters over it that there wasn't an inch of glass left showing. When it took me twenty seconds to find the door handle, and another ten to get the key into the lock, my opinion of the poster-plasterer took a nose dive. Hemlock's smug face staring at me from every single glossy sheet did nothing to improve it.

"Hemlock!" I yelled when the door finally opened and I walked inside the very dark shop. There was a sudden rush of movement as many small furry animals fled into the shadows and out of the cat flap. Erebus trotted up to me and leant against my legs, shooting me a look that promised none of this was his idea. "But you could have kept them under control, or kicked them out!" I countered. The hellhound just shot me another plaintive look, the meaning of which was abundantly obvious.

Keeping Hemlock under control was a fool's task.

"Where have you been? I needed your help," Hemlock complained from his place on the shop counter.

"You needed my help?" I repeated, forgetting I was angry for a second. Even though he was supposed to be my partner - my familiar - Hemlock seldom asked for help with anything. He either ordered or coerced.

"Yes, you've got thumbs. The posters could have gone up far more efficiently if you'd been here. I had to do everything myself. Is this how you support your familiar? Abandoning me in my time of need? This could be great for us, Hazel. We could have power over everyone in town! I know it's a role reversal to have the familiar in the driving seat, but I think it's quite clear which one of us has the real potential in this partnership…"

"I thought you hated the idea of being a protest vote?" I interrupted, knowing that there was zero point arguing with Hemlock over his insane ambitions.

"Oh, you mean the posters? 'Fed up of liars and losers? Protest by voting Hemlock for Mayor!' he quoted. I thought about it and decided it wasn't a bad idea. Half of this town thinks I'm a regular cat, so this is for them. The other half might have heard of me by reputation, but their own familiars will bring them around to the right side," he said, preening his whiskers.

"Which is your side," I couldn't help but observe dryly.

"What do you think about pom-poms?" Hemlock said, abruptly changing the subject.

"Pom…what?"

"With my face on. Every time someone comes into the shop, you could do a short cheer that lists my best points and then wave them in customers' faces. It would be very memorable."

"It would be very annoying."

"Excellent!" Hemlock said, apparently deciding I'd

agreed to it. "Did you see the secret regret from my past I posted?"

"I haven't read all of them yet," I confessed.

"Why not? Don't you care what keeps me up at night, agonising over a past I can't change?" When I didn't respond, he sulked for a second before continuing. "My secret past regret was that I regret not taking advantage of the power vacuum in this town when we returned after dispatching the last mayor. I could have made myself mayor back then and saved all of this fuss and bother." He blinked and glanced at me. "Pretty good, right? It's something I've never told anyone, something I regret, and also absolutely selfless and sincere, because it would have saved the lives of the idiots running in this election, who wouldn't have been murdered." He wiped away a pretend tear. "I bet the mystery murderer was touched."

"I think you're very lucky that your campaign posters make it clear you're a cat," I informed him. "Are you sure you want to be mayor? I didn't think you were very serious about this, but you really seem to be. I'm actually impressed by your commitment," I confessed, surprising myself and my familiar at the same time. "I just want to make sure you know what you're getting into."

He rubbed his furry chin. "It might be fun for a bit. If it goes wrong, or I get bored, I know it will be okay."

"Oh?" I said, raising an eyebrow and feeling like this explanation was probably not going to be a good one, coming from the wannabe mayor with the attention span of a toothpick.

"It'll be fine because I've got you, and you'll know what to do. You're great at solving problems. You can be my vice mayor and take over when I don't feel like it anymore."

"I think that's very nearly a compliment," I said, knowing I had to take what I could get.

"It was nearly intended that way," Hemlock replied. We looked at each other for a long moment, feeling like we were finally reading from the same page in a book for the first time in a very long time.

It was a touching moment, which was probably why Jesse Heathen chose that moment to ruin it. The apothecary door swung open and he marched in with all of the flourish of the star of a sitcom making their entrance. Mine and Hemlock's little heart to heart ended and the usual chaos resumed.

"Rival! How dare you come in here? To my headquarters? He's trying to steal secrets! Get him out!" Hemlock hissed, fluffing up and glaring at Jesse.

"I suppose he's accusing me of spying, isn't he?" Jesse said, having known Hemlock for much longer than I had and clearly recognising the signs and the attitude.

"Why are you here?" I asked him, taking Hemlock's side for once.

"Spying," Hemlock hissed.

"I wanted to make sure you're okay. Seeing something like that can't have been easy," Jesse said, his amber eyes going all wide and understanding.

"Where was your concern the first time it happened?" I asked, distinctly unimpressed with this new, caring act.

"Well, you know what they say... the first headless body is bad, but it's the second that gets to you."

"Do they say that?" I raised my eyebrows.

"Well, they should!" Jesse said, moving around me to lean on the shop counter. He thought better of it when Hemlock raised a spiky paw.

"I'm surprised they let you go so soon," I told him.

Jesse shrugged and examined my weekly tea special stand. This week it was *Luminosi-Tea* - a tea for bright thoughts and ideas. "They had their hands pretty full. In any case, I arrived *after* the action and no one can place me at the scene of the crime, because I created a shadow self to hang around at home. Sean's super obvious plainclothes officers will have seen me at home at the time the crime was being committed. I dissolved it when I left for the library."

I noticed that Jesse didn't say where he'd actually been prior to that.

"Anyway, just make sure you stay focused on the case. I have every faith that you will solve it. Although, if there was a delay, I would understand," Jesse said, the sympathetic expression back on his face.

"What, so more of your political rivals can be bumped off?"

A wolfish grin jumped onto his lips. "I could be in danger, too," he said, trying to pretend that I hadn't hit the nail on the head.

"We both know that's unlikely. Are you sure you're not the one responsible for the deaths?"

"You know it's not my style. Far too messy. Really, Hazel, you shouldn't be so suspicious. I'm just here to make sure you're okay, wish you well with the mystery solving, and ask what you think about the secrets being kept by an important person that we both know."

"One of the ones that was posted in the blog comments tonight? I didn't see anything groundbreaking," I said, wondering what it was that Jesse thought I should have noticed.

"No, not those secrets, if you can even call them that. I know I said Graham's was the worst, but in truth, if I were the angel of justice, I'd probably have closed my eyes and picked one at random. I deal in secrets, and they were all rubbish and insincere. Not like the one that someone else close to you is keeping."

I stiffened and gave him my full attention. "Are you talking about Sean?"

"It's interesting that your mind went there first."

"You wanted it to go there," I countered, annoyed that he was getting under my skin already.

He shrugged, an easy smile on his lips. "You're right, but now that we are on the topic… I happened to hear something interesting about our mutual friend, DCI Admiral. Apparently, he lives in some rather fancy digs. Word on the street is that there's quite a story behind how he got the place. I'm never one to judge on appearances, but living in something that by all accounts sounds like a small castle doesn't sound like Sean Admiral's style, does it? I suppose there's more to him than meets the eye. He's probably shown you around and told you all about it already though, right? I found out about this months ago and wrote you a letter at the time, fully intending to return to Wormwood, but time gets away from us all, doesn't it? I'm probably just sharing old news."

"I've been to his house," I said, choosing my words very carefully.

"He invited you there?"

Darn it. Jesse was good with words. I should have known better. Devils were the masters of details, especially when the details were in the deals they made - which were inevitably to their advantage. "Sean's a busy man and I work a lot, too. It's convenient for us to meet at my place."

Jesse raised his eyebrows and said nothing. He also knew that silence was the best way to get someone to keep talking and spill their own secrets.

Even though I knew exactly what he was doing, I still couldn't help myself from attempting to put him straight. "We haven't been dating that long really, in the grand scheme of things, and it's hard to find the time to have deep, personal chats. We're always busy trying to solve crimes. He'll tell me whatever it is you think you know about him when he's ready, and I'm okay with that."

"Are you really?" Jesse said, not believing my words for a second. Clearly, I wasn't cut out to be a politician. He ran a finger along a shelf whilst he pretended to decide whether or not to say the thing he'd been building up to saying ever since he'd entered the shop. "I can't stay silent. It's my duty to share this news with you," he said, deliberately going against my wishes. "The way I heard it, Sean got his house from the victim of a crime. He solved a crime that was committed against a woman. She was so impressed that she changed her will. Unfortunately, she died fairly soon after doing that and under some pretty mysterious circumstances," Jesse said, not making eye contact with me at any point during this speech.

"Mysterious circumstances?" I ground out, knowing that it was exactly what he wanted me to ask, but I was curious in spite of it.

"The criminal responsible for the first crime was accidentally released from prison on day release. He returned to the victim's house and murdered her, before disappearing forever… leaving Sean in line for a big inheritance." Jesse finally looked at me more seriously, having enjoyed everything up to this point. "I'm not suggesting that Sean was responsible for letting a dangerous criminal go free, or for persuading the victim that her will should include him, but clearly, he accepted his bequeathment. He's now living in a place few police officers could dream of being able to afford. I think he was left a tidy sum of money, too, but that's by the by."

"Why are you telling me all of this?" I pressed, torn between wanting to kick Jesse out of the door and that horrible feeling of cold dread that accompanied the suspicions I'd already had that Sean wasn't telling me something - something that seemed like it might be really important. If what Jesse was saying was true, I couldn't think of a good reason why Sean had kept it from me. However, I also knew that the devil loved to stir up trouble. Everything he said should be taken with a fistful of salt, let alone a pinch.

"I have no hidden agenda, in case you're wondering. It's nothing to do with me. I just heard some information on my travels, and as a concerned friend, I thought I would pass it on to you. You and Sean have become very close while I've been out of town. I'm happy for you, Hazel, but I also think you should make sure that the man you seem to like so much is being completely honest with you."

"I'm sure he has his reasons," I bit back, feeling cornered.

"I'm sure he does, but ask yourself this… if he's serious about the way he feels about you, why would he keep something like this a secret? And what else might he be hiding?"

I took a deep breath, hoping that some brilliant comeback would jump into my head, and I could send Jesse and his troublemaking tongue packing. Unfortunately, all I could think was that the devil had a point. After all of the trials we'd gone through together - and with the evidence of how deep, dark secrets invariably led to a horrible fate all around us - I just couldn't think of a logical explanation for Sean's silence. If what Jesse had said was true, I wanted to know why he hadn't told me about it.

I wanted to know why Sean was still keeping secrets.

11

THE GREAT DEBATE

Even though the scenes in Wormwood's library should have been enough to give anyone nightmares, the reason I tossed and turned that night was because of Jesse's words. I woke up the next morning without the benefit of a good night's sleep and with a thundercloud over my head.

"Good morning, Hazel. Did you sleep well?" Aunt Minerva asked, looking up from the cup of coffee she'd made herself.

I managed to smile at the new head of the Witch Council, but it was an effort that was apparently all too noticeably made. "How is everything going? It's nice that you're back home," I managed, speaking of my aunt's recent long absences.

She sighed dramatically in response, but her focus remained on me. "Has something happened?"

"You haven't heard about the murders?" I asked, plonking myself down at the kitchen table and feeling the thundercloud sink lower still.

"Linda did mention something about that when I

bumped into her on my way in last night, as she was sneaking down for a midnight snack. I'm sure you'll help Sean the way you always do. He has a lot of faith in you. We all do," she said, gently fishing for the real problem and trying some words of reassurance to see if they helped.

"It's Jesse Heathen that's bothering me. Last night, he said some things about Sean, and I don't know how much of it was true. Some of it's probably true. Jesse doesn't actually lie that often, but he is very good at leaving out the most important details," I explained, knowing it was unfair to keep her guessing.

"Most problems can be resolved if you address them directly… through conversation."

I nodded, knowing my pragmatic aunt was right. "There will be a conversation at some point. There has to be. Unfortunately, right now, there's no good time for it to happen, and Jesse told me what he did last night because he knows that's the case and he wanted to get under my skin and cause trouble… and I'm really annoyed that it's worked!" I sighed, letting the frustration flow out of me when I spoke the real issue out loud.

Minerva threw me a long, cool look and I was acutely aware of the differences between my aunts. Linda would have patted my hand or given me a hug. Minerva was far less warm and fuzzy, but far more useful when it came to advice. "You know that you've given Jesse permission to make you feel this way by not talking to Sean sooner. I sincerely doubt that you were completely in the dark about what Jesse revealed to you. You're no fool, Hazel, and I'm sure you had your reasons to not get to the bottom of whatever it is that Jesse has dangled in front of you, but it seems to me that you have two problems. The first should be simple enough to resolve by talking to Sean, instead of torturing yourself over possibilities. The second will involve you deciding how you feel about Jesse, because I think one, or both of you, might not be fully decided on the matter."

My eyebrows flew up. "How I feel about Jesse? I feel that he's a pain in the behind! Things in Wormwood were better when he wasn't in town. I'm not saying he's completely responsible for what is going on right now, or even the times in the past, but he certainly influences events, and never in a good way!" I looked up at my aunt and saw that her eyebrows were also lifted, questioning me over the things I'd left unsaid. I felt a knot grow in my stomach.

"Logic can't be applied to everything," she said, taking a sip of her coffee and looking wise and knowledgable.

I clamped down on my urge to remind my aunt that both she and her sister didn't have a successful relationship with the opposite sex between them, so dishing out wisdom on that topic seemed a bit rich. If I said anything like that, it would basically be acknowledging that there was something between me and Jesse that had grown like an unnoticed weed during the time that he'd been away from Wormwood, only revealing itself when he'd come back.

And there definitely wasn't anything like that. Was there?

"What are you planning to do about all of those posters?" my aunt asked, wisely changing the subject.

"Posters?" I queried, before I remembered exactly which posters she was referring to and also why it was strangely dark in the kitchen this morning. I glared at the shop window, which remained completely blacked out. After Jesse's visit last night, I'd gone straight to bed in a huff, forgetting about Hemlock's antics. "Is there a spell to poof it all away?" I asked, hoping that there would be a non-labour intensive alternative available to magic users who were good at getting spells to work reliably for them.

"There are cleaning spells, but by the time you looked one up and convinced it to work, you could have finished cleaning the window by hand," she said, sharing what I'd already known deep down.

"I'd better get peeling and scrubbing. What are the chances that he used something more permanent than wallpaper paste to stick them up?" I said rhetorically, walking towards my manual labour filled morning.

"Do you think he's serious about this?" Minerva called after me.

It took me a couple of moments to work out who she was talking about.

"Hemlock? Yes, I think he is. Well, he's serious about winning. He seems to be under the impression that after he wins and gets bored with the job, I'll take over as his vice mayor, or something like that."

"Do you think he has a chance?"

That question made me hesitate for longer. Longer than it would have done normally, because now that Minerva was the leader of the Witch Council, this conversation felt a touch more dangerous. It was her job to stop the abuse of magic, and abuse of magic was basically Hemlock's middle name. If he became mayor, he'd have even more opportunity to do things that the Council would not approve of. "I'm not actually sure. Stranger things have happened in Wormwood," I said lightly.

Aunt Minerva considered my words. "In that case, I think I might move to Oxford before this town becomes a cat-led dictatorship."

I had to look really carefully at her face to see if she was joking.

I still wasn't completely sure.

* * *

My day had only got worse when Sean had called to remind me that there was a debate happening in the local church hall, and the official press representative (me) should be there to cover it and watch out for any suspicious behaviour after the events of the previous evening.

"I assumed that would be cancelled!" I'd replied, still trying to scrape poster remnants off the glass, whilst I'd held the walkabout shop phone to my ear with my shoulder. Hemlock had used superglue to put his posters up. It was no wonder he'd made himself scarce this morning.

Sean had sighed, sounding about as tired as I felt. "The surviving candidates discussed the matter online last night in their group chat, after Andy shared the statement I wrote for him to share. It would have been irresponsible to hold back information about what happened in the library when it could affect the safety of the other candidates. They spoke together and collectively felt that the debate and the election itself should continue, because the victims would have wanted democracy to prevail, for the hopeful mayors to show no fear, and for their own memories to be preserved. You get the gist of it."

"I think so," I'd agreed, cynically thinking that they'd used almost every cliché in the book to justify doing something that they all wanted to do for personal reasons, but making it seem like it had a deeper, more respectful purpose.

It was only when I saw Sean standing outside the church hall that Jesse's words from the previous evening rushed back into my head, escaping the mental box I'd finally managed to shove them inside when I'd been poster scraping. My heart quickened and my palms grew sweaty as I steeled myself in preparation for walking over to the

DCI and asking him about his house. My aunt was right. The best thing to do was not agonise over what could or might be, and to come right out and ask Sean for the truth.

"It's about to start. We've got to go in immediately," he greeted me, his eyes searching the surroundings behind me, as if he expected the killer to pop up from one of the landscaped bushes at any second. "I'm on my own today. The rest of the team is still working on last night's crime scene. I'm hoping that the reduced police presence might make the killer relax, or even make them wonder if we're focusing on someone outside of the candidate pool."

"Are we?" I asked, wondering if I'd missed a big development after leaving last night.

"No. All of the signs point to this being someone who is obsessed with the question of who will become mayor, and is therefore directly involved in the process. They may be hiding behind a facade of wanting everyone to tell the truth, but their motives are undoubtedly darker," Sean said, sharing his lack of faith in human nature. "It could be someone who doesn't believe that they have what it takes to win the election the traditional way."

A couple of people jumped into my mind when he said that. Question marks hovered by their names, but I stayed silent. It was only a theory, and we both knew it.

"It could be something else. A grudge or vendetta that we don't know about yet," Sean added, mirroring my own thoughts.

We simply didn't know enough, but it was equally true that we weren't going to learn anything more by standing around outside the church hall hypothesising when all of the action was inside.

"Do you think they'll have snacks?" I said when we turned to go inside. Sean looked at me. "You know... like small bowls of salted peanuts on tables?" He kept looking at me, like I'd sprouted another head. "Well, they should," I said, huffy that political debates didn't come with snacks supplied.

I bit my lip when we entered the hall and joined the throng of people who'd come to shout questions and judge the answers of those who aspired to one day be the mayor of this town. Jesse's words were still heavy in my heart, but I hadn't avoided talking about the issue with Sean - there just hadn't been time. It was a bad excuse to kick down the road, but I would make sure that there was time very soon indeed and not put off the conversation forever.

Sean and I took our seats at the back at the same moment a ripple of applause broke out to welcome the candidates to the stage. The surviving five took their seats, the temporary stage creaking as they moved around. The only candidate absent was Hemlock. A chair had been put out for him and a PR photo placed on the seat.

I could only assume that Hemlock himself had submitted the photo, which I had never seen before. It looked like it had been taken at the sort of glamour photoshoot session that had been popular in the eighties and nineties. Hemlock appeared to have had a blow dry and he'd also managed to make his eyes wide and innocent looking, glowing with starlight. I silently wondered who the photographer had been and how Hemlock had managed to interact with them. I silently decided that some things were better left a mystery.

Anita Heron trotted out when the candidates had settled, looking about as comfortable as a porcupine in a cocktail sausage factory. "I'm sure by now everyone in this room has heard about the terrible incident that occurred in Wormwood's library yesterday evening. Our thoughts and prayers are with all of those who were close to the victim. The candidates wished for this scheduled hustings to continue, as they will not be cowed by the threats of an unknown individual. I think that is very courageous of all of them and deserves a round of applause," she finished, glancing down at her note cards to make sure she'd said that part correctly. Clapping followed and the candidates nodded appreciatively. Anita cleared her throat again, noticing that she had one more line to say. "I have been notified that one of our candidates will not be partaking in today's discussion. The reason give for his absence is that, being a cat, his counterarguments would be impossible for normal humans to understand," she read out without any trace of humour whatsoever.

The audience let out a huge 'Awwwww' and I heard several people sitting nearby comment on how cute and fluffy the cat looked and how proud his owner must be.

"More like mortified," I muttered through gritted teeth. Sean reached out and squeezed my hand in solidarity, but I thought his mouth was turning up at the corners.

"He's got my vote. A cat would do the job a lot better than any of these fools," someone else close by said, sending a shiver down my spine. Something told me that the owner of that voice might not be alone in their thinking - especially after all of the drama that had surrounded proceedings so far. If too many shared his opinion, things may end very badly for Wormwood - a place where even voting for the token fluffy animal could result in the town being turned into a post-apocalyptic wasteland.

"May I take the opportunity to begin this debate by thanking the Witchwood Police Force for the work they have done thus far," Jesse said, standing up and nabbing the microphone from Anita. As soon as he began speaking, all eyes were on him and there was sudden and absolute silence. Everyone wanted to hear every word he said. It didn't hurt that he was doing his usual trick of adding some sort of devilish glamour to his words. I frowned and folded my arms, tempted to pull a bucket out of the in-between and throw cold water over him. The killer had already made it very clear that they didn't approve of cheating, so Jesse's audacity was astounding. "Having said that, it is my belief that last night also highlighted one of the most important issues that the next Mayor of Wormwood must address - our lack of policing."

Sean sat up straight and frowned. Hadn't Jesse just been thanking him for his hard work?

The aspiring mayor walked across to the other side of the stage, looking like he belonged there, looking like he thrived on attention. "We are fortunate that Witchwood has such an excellent police force. I know that they have helped our town many times during the past year, and for that, we are all very grateful. I don't mean this as a slight against them, or a comment on their work. Quite the opposite. I think that they should be looked up to and become something that Wormwood can aspire to have... with its own police force."

"You want to open a police station in Wormwood?" someone called out from the audience, right on cue. I frowned, silently thinking that Jesse was definitely not above planting audience members to further his own arguments and support him in this debate.

"I do," he confirmed, smiling a bright white smile. "Wormwood is a wonderful town, but it is also a growing town. When places become larger and more people visit - for example, through the tourism which as mayor I would continue to encourage - crime tends to rise as well. It's an unfortunate side effect, but one that can't be ignored. We can't be calling Witchwood every time someone swipes a bun from the local bakery, can we? That is why, when I'm

Mayor of Wormwood, I will push to open a police station in town, so we will never need to call Witchwood for help again. Their wonderful police officers can go back to focusing on their own town, and we will have a police presence on our streets, offering help to the community and creating a happier, safer town for all who live and work here."

Applause exploded in the room and Jesse's smile grew brighter still. He'd kicked off the debate by raising an issue that no one had even been speaking about prior to today, and now it seemed like a great idea. The rest of the candidates would either have to back an idea that no one could ever deny had been Jesse's, or come out against it, when there was already a huge amount of vocal support in favour.

"Game, set, match," Sean said by my side, agreeing with my own judgement.

"I don't think turning Wormwood into a police state is a good idea," Andy Carat said, standing up from his seat and projecting his voice. Anita rushed over to hand him a second microphone. "The residents of Wormwood are not afraid. Why bring people into this town, who will boss everyone around and make law-abiding people afraid to go about their daily business? A neighbourhood watch scheme would be far more friendly, and quite frankly, far more effective."

Jesse raised his eyebrows, visibly pleased that he'd dragged someone into this debate with him. "I'm sure you'd make a great neighbourhood watch leader. I hear that you're rather handy with an axe, so should any drastic steps need to be taken..."

A great murmuring broke out in the room at the mention of Andy being skilled with a weapon - especially a weapon that was traditionally used to remove heads from bodies. I glanced at Sean, but I knew that Andy's claim about the specifics of the weapon used in last night's murder was not something that would have been released to the public yet - not before a pathologist could confirm it.

"Mr Heathen is trying to bait all of you," Andy told the audience. "He is referring to my success as a competitive wood-chopping champion. It's a fun hobby of mine and nothing more sinister than that."

"I'm sure we all believe you and don't find it at all suspicious that you're an expert with an axe when there has been a slew of beheadings," Jesse said, struggling to keep the delight from his voice.

"Well... she makes axes!" Andy spluttered, pointing at Jade Rey in an attempt to deflect scrutiny away from himself.

"Are you saying that she *supplied* you with an axe?"

Andy was making it way too easy for Jesse.

Ten minutes later, it was obvious that no one was going to emerge from this hustings untainted. No one, except perhaps for Hemlock - whose decision not to show up now seemed like a masterstroke. I frowned. Even though Hemlock's point about not being able to communicate was a valid one, I was surprised that he wasn't hanging around somewhere, eating a bag of popcorn and enjoying his rivals ripping each other to shreds.

I was surprised he hadn't done anything to make the carnage worse.

It probably meant he was causing carnage elsewhere.

The back of my neck itched when I wondered where he was right this second and what he might be planning. I tried to let my anxiety go. For all I knew, Hemlock had found a new reality television show and was watching couples get all smoochy on a mediterranean island whilst all of this was taking place. I was probably worrying over nothing.

I'd just convinced myself that Hemlock genuinely was elsewhere when the doors of the hall burst open, hitting the back walls with a bang. A collective gasp went around the room, as everyone immediately thought of the axe wielding maniac, but it wasn't a marauding murderer who'd caused the doors to burst open… it was a sea of furry bodies.

"Plague!"

"Earthquake!"

Voices shouted in panic as the surge of animals whispered around their legs. There was a fluttering sound and suddenly there was paper in the air, released by the stampeding familiars. One of the postcard-sized colourful rectangles fell into my lap and I read what had been printed on it.

Hate the debate? Vote Hemlock for mayor!

"Great timing," Sean commented, having received a flyer of his own. "The hat is really something, too," he added, talking about the fez that my familiar had opted to wear for this particular publicity photo.

"Where is he getting all of this stuff from?" I hissed, making a mental note to immediately contact the printer who produced my magazine for me. Something told me I might have run up quite a large bill on someone else's behalf without being aware of it.

As the last papers fell upon heads or laps and the confusion waned, Hemlock himself was carried in on a shield, supported by six other cats. He'd got himself a new crown and cape (the first crown and cape he'd owned had met their end in the Himalayas). All eyes were on the cat parade when he was carried up to the stage and set down at the centre with great ceremony.

With a trembling hand, Anita took the microphone back from Andy Carat and lowered it towards the waiting cat.

Hemlock took a deep breath, puffing out his chest and then...

Mew.

It sounded like a kitten asking its owner to give it one more treat.

It was an utterly ridiculous noise for a fully grown cat to make.

The audience loved it.

"Vote Hemlock!" someone yelled.

"Hemlock for mayor!" another followed.

"Who cares about policing? We need a cat for mayor! That will bring in the tourists!" someone else shouted. There were cheers of agreement - more than I remembered there being in support of Jesse's big idea at the start of the debate.

I looked away from my devious familiar to another devilish face on the left hand side of the stage, wondering if he realised his greatest rival was a cat. Jesse didn't look perturbed by Hemlock's appearance and vocal supporters. He wasn't actually looking at my familiar at all, but directly back at me with a questioning look on his face. His eyes flickered to my left, before returning to meet my gaze again. He tilted his head and raised his eyebrows. I felt my own expression darken.

Jesse was enquiring whether I'd talked to Sean yet.

And I'd just revealed that I hadn't.

"What's he so smug about?" Sean asked, having noticed Jesse laughing to himself on stage whilst the bedlam continued all around us.

"I think he just enjoys trouble - caused by him or anyone else," I said through gritted teeth, reaching out for Sean's arm and focusing all of my attention on him. Jesse was going to be sorely disappointed if he thought I was going to let this new game of his drag on. "I need to talk to you about something important."

Sean looked surprised, but he followed me out of the church hall and into the light drizzle that had set in. "What did you want to tell me? Have you worked out something about the murder?" he asked, his face tight with worry.

"Oh, no, it's not about that," I said, suddenly feeling ridiculous for raising a subject that wasn't relevant to the very serious serial killer investigation. "It's something else. I, uh… I've been wondering about your house." I floundered, struck by how ridiculous I sounded and failing to say the words I'd planned in my head over and over again last night when I hadn't slept.

"My house? What about it?" Sean asked, looking nonplussed. He glanced back towards the church hall, making it obvious that he didn't think this warranted missing the killer's next move.

He probably had a point.

I'd definitely allowed Jesse to get to me, but that didn't mean I should back out now. I might be the maker of my own problem, but I also needed to be the solver. "I know this isn't the best time to bring it up, but I was wondering how you came to have the house and how long you've lived there for?" I tried to keep my expression open, not wanting to sound like I was accusing my boyfriend of anything. Inside, I was in turmoil - uncertain about truths that might have been kept from me and the many possible reasons why Sean might have stayed silent.

I hoped I wouldn't have to wonder any longer.

"It was left to me in a will. I've only been living there for a few years. What is it you want to know?" A crease appeared between his eyebrows.

"I suppose I really want to know why you've never invited me to your house," I said, treading a careful line between probing and parroting what Jesse had said to me.

Sean scratched his head and looked away. "I thought you were happy with us always meeting at your place. You can come over any time. I'm not hiding any skeletons in my closets."

The way he said the last part so seriously made me wonder all over again. And then I knew I couldn't stay silent about what I knew and risk retaining even the smallest flicker of doubt. "Jesse told me that he heard you were given the house by a woman who was the victim of a crime that you solved. She was then murdered, and with her will legally altered, the place went to you," I confessed, shooting Sean a guilty look.

My boyfriend froze, his grey eyes as cold as the Arctic sea. "You're letting Jesse interfere with our relationship? He's been back here for five minutes, and already, he can't leave you alone." Sean's teeth ground together.

"What? I didn't let him interfere with anything," I protested. "He just passed on some information. Look - is it true? I really want to know the whole story because I am not stupid enough to believe that Jesse Heathen was being completely honest with me. That's why I came straight to you for the real answers." I opened my eyes wide, imploring him to see how my hand had been forced, and how I didn't mean this as an attack upon his honour. The problem was, some boxes can't be shut again after they've been opened. A woman named Pandora would back me up on that one.

There was a long silence, during which Sean avoided making eye contact. "I don't need any more of your help today. You can go home," he said after an incredibly long silence. Then, he spun on his heel and re-entered the church hall, shutting the door behind him without saying goodbye.

12

CLEANING UP

Sean wasn't telling me something.

After Jesse's bombshell, I'd remained convinced that there would be a good explanation for everything and that the devil was twisting things in his usual manner. Now, I wasn't so sure. After the town hall debate disaster, I'd spent the rest of the day replaying my conversation with Sean, and then a good part of the night, too. By the following morning, I was seriously sleep deprived and deep down a rabbit hole of endless possibilities that Sean had done nothing to rescue me from. His silence felt like confirmation. But confirmation of what?

I stumbled down the stairs, rubbing my puffy eyes and hoping that someone had put a pot of coffee on. Coffee might at least take some of the sting out of the prospect of the day ahead.

What I got was a face full of smoke.

"What's happening? Is there a fire?" I managed to choke out, before the smoke got in my throat and I started coughing. I reached into the in-between, fumbling about for something that I hoped would be a fire hose complete with a water source.

"It's okay! The smoke will go in a second!" Aunt Linda called out.

"What is going on?" I shouted a second later when the dense cloud had become a lot more hazy.

"Nothing to worry about, just some normal spell work!"

I took advantage of the lingering smoke to pull several faces that couldn't be seen. "What sort of spell work?" I asked, managing to make it to the bottom of the stairs. The smoke made me feel like I was about to find myself on stage singing a song and pretending to be a pop star. I shook away the memories of a bygone age of television. What was taking place in the kitchen was far more dastardly than Cheryl from Basildon, who fancied herself as a Kylie Minogue duplicate.

I blinked the stars from my eyes.

"Don't worry about it," Linda said. There was the suspicious sound of many things being swept off the table, as someone desperately tried to cover up some evidence. Unfortunately for my aunt, in her haste to cover things up, a piece of the spell had escaped. I bent down and picked up the pink heart made from rice paper. It looked like it had been spiked with liquid of some kind because there was a darker stain at its centre.

"A love spell? Why would you want to do a love spell?" I asked, looking up at my aunt, now that the smoke had finally cleared.

She dropped the black plastic bin bag she'd just pushed all of the leftover ingredients into onto the floor, peeved that she'd been found out. "No reason. For fun, I suppose." She sat down by the table and poked the cauldron that still bubbled, releasing the aroma of rue, pepper, and lemons.

"It's because I'm bored, Hazel! I run the shop for you when you're busy, and that's fine, but here I am, in the prime of my life... don't say it!" she said when my eyebrows shot up at that claim "...And there is literally no one who's single in this town! There's no one dateable! When Minerva was always around, it wasn't so bad. Then there were two of us all alone in this world. That's all changed now. She's busy with her powerful job, where people fawn over her day in and day out, and the only thing I have melting over me is ice-cream." Linda looked rather pleased with herself over that analogy.

"Who are you planning to give this to if there aren't any eligible bachelors around?" I asked, holding up the rice paper heart.

"Great question!" Aunt Linda said, smiling and pointing at me, like she was a university professor giving a lecture. "I am making cupcakes using a recipe from Tristan that I've tweaked a bit. I'm going to put the hearts on top and they're also inside of the cakes themselves, just in case my targets pick off the heart on the top. Not everyone likes eating rice paper. I mean, let's be honest, it's definitely not the best part of a cake, is it? It looks great though and gives the cakes a touch of class."

"Aunt Linda!" I protested, hoping to get her back on track.

"Right, yes... the cupcakes are masquerading as a promotion for a new mail order cupcake business. I have a list of top businessmen who are single and not too hideously ugly. I'm going to send all of them a cupcake as a free sample. They eat the cupcake and - bingo! They will be struck by a sudden strange desire to contact the baker of the cupcakes, and I'll have dates with some wealthy and powerful men." She sighed happily.

"Do you really think that wealthy and powerful businessmen will eat an unsolicited cupcake that's been sent through the post to them?" I asked, curious about my aunt's thinking, or the lack of it.

Linda shrugged. "I figured if I sent enough of them out, someone's got to be stupid enough to try one. Anyway, who would poison someone by a mail order cupcake sample? It's so suspicious that it can't be suspicious. It's the good old double cake bluff, but with love potion, not poison."

"Can't you just try online dating?" I asked, feeling more exhausted than I had when I'd woken up after hearing such a longwinded plan.

"Online what now?" Aunt Linda said looking curious.

"Dating?" I said, tilting my head. "You do know that there are mobile phone apps as well as websites where you can upload photos of yourself and find single men, who are actually looking to start a relationship?"

Aunt Linda frowned. "You can use your phone for that? The last time I looked it was all internet chatrooms where serial killers hung out, waiting to strike lonely women. Everyone was warned not to meet up with strangers. When you're my age, I suppose it's easy to dwell in the past and miss these new developments," she said, making a rare allusion to her impressively advanced years. They might not show on her face, but years wore themselves into your spirit, like the shine on a well-frequented step.

"There's a big wide world out there. If you can find a decent internet connection in Wormwood, you won't need those cupcakes," I told her.

Aunt Linda was still looking shellshocked. "I can't believe it." She shook herself. "There are some finished cupcakes on top of the oven. Help yourself. Ignore any strange feelings of affection you might develop for me after eating them."

I walked over to the coffee pot and shot the cakes a dubious look. They did look tempting, but the idea of deliberately ingesting a love potion was off-putting in the extreme. "Have you also thought about maybe starting a mail order cupcake business for real? Some of the best evil schemes can become business ideas," I said, before wondering what I was talking about. Had Hemlock rubbed off on me?

"I suppose I could do with a project," Aunt Linda said, tapping her chin and looking thoughtful. "You probably shouldn't eat those cupcakes by the way. I tried everything I could to make the potion taste better, but it's still rather noticeable."

"By the way, have you seen Hemlock?" I asked Aunt Linda, pouring myself some coffee.

"No, but he was supposed to be helping me with this spell. That was our deal. He wrote it down, so I could understand him. If I helped him with his money spell, then he would help me with this one. I suppose I should have known better than to trust him."

"I wonder what he's up to?" I mused, my mind once again whispering that my familiar was taking something more seriously and going to greater lengths than I'd previously imagined him capable of, and I should probably pay more attention and launch an intervention. Unfortunately, it was at that moment that the shop door swung open and Sean walked in.

He looked sheepish in the extreme.

"Good morning. I was, uh, walking around town, canvassing for witnesses and I thought I would drop in for a visit."

"Would you like a cupcake?" my aunt asked, gesturing to the pink frosted creations sitting on top of the oven.

"Don't," I said to Sean, shooting my aunt a warning look.

She flashed an innocent smile back at me, before walking up the stairs. If anyone needs me, I'll be online searching for Mr Right. And Mr Wrong, too, if he's on there. I'm open to trying a few out before settling."

"What's going on?" Sean said when she'd gone. "Why can't I have a cupcake?"

"Do you really want one?" I asked, genuinely curious about the idea of Sean willingly eating something so very pink and sparkly.

"I…" He frowned. "No, probably not. It smells strange in here. Was there a fire?"

"Why are you here?" I asked him, knowing that the conversation had to turn serious at some point. I led him into the shop and further away from any listening ears that might be straining down the stairs, hoping to pick up on gossip.

"Yesterday, I shouldn't have walked away," Sean said, his pained expression giving way to words that came spilling out in a rush. "I can only imagine what that must have made you think of me. I thought about it for the rest of the day and I realised how wrong it is to have kept this from you for so long. We're together and I want to share everything with you. I don't have any excuses, but I want to make it up to you now by telling you everything about the house where I live." He sucked air in through his teeth, pausing as he gathered his thoughts.

I felt my heart beat a little faster in my chest. Jesse's stories swirled in my head and Sean's own words sat heavy in the air. What had Sean done to inherit his property? Was there something terrible that I didn't know about the man I loved that might change everything about our relationship and the way I felt? I didn't think it was possible, but that didn't stop the doubts from rising up and shaking me.

"I don't know how Jesse got his claws into all of this, but I want to make it right," Sean said, fury flashing in his grey eyes for a second, before he calmed again and the oceanic stillness returned. "It all started with a theft," he began.

I sat back and listened as Sean explained everything.

"Lisa Farrow was the victim of an unusual robbery. It was a robbery that involved the theft of several items from her house. An old umbrella stand, a rapier hanging on the wall, and a crystal goblet were taken, whilst other valuables remained in place." He paused and pushed his hair back from his forehead, the short strands immediately springing back into the same position. "It was a strange case, but not anything particularly serious. As it happened, I chanced upon the entrance and exit strategy of the thief through an overlooked window and managed to direct the crime scene investigation officers to search there for evidence. They found several fingerprints. As it happened, those prints were on file, having been collected from the scene of a much more serious crime several counties away. It was a murder that had occurred after a robbery."

He sat back in his chair. "Obviously, that changed how we treated this crime. It was fortunate that we did alter our approach, because the next night the thief returned and was apprehended carrying a machete. It would be speculation to say whether he definitely intended to murder Lisa Farrow that night, and his motive for doing so was also unclear to me at the time. The best guess I had was that it was some sort of fetish thing. The murderer takes some items without the victim being able to stop him from gaining access to the house, revelling in the power it gives him. Later, he returns to finish the job.

Kind of like a ritual. At least, that was what I thought it was all about, back before I knew anything about magic. To be fair, Lisa Farrow never put me right at the time." His lips thinned as he considered his long history of crime solving and all of the occasions where there was a question mark in his mind over whether he'd got it right, or if the true motive and even guilty party had slipped him by.

"I know you've always done the best you can," I said, reaching out and patting Sean's hand. I knew it wasn't much comfort and doubt would always reign in the police officer's mind, now that he knew what he knew about the existence of magic. In my case, I only had a short writing career to be a little bit embarrassed about, but Sean's problems were a lot more consequential. Fates could have been changed and lives affected. He had to live with that.

"Anyway, it was great that we'd managed to catch the crook. There was enough evidence to put him away for a very long time indeed."

"That's why she changed her will?" I asked, sensing that Jesse had been telling me the truth, just not all of it.

Sean nodded. "I advised her that it was inappropriate and that I couldn't accept. She told me that she had no heirs to pass her property and fortune on to, and that she felt she owed me a great debt. I said she needed to find a better person to inherit it all in the many long years of her life I was sure she had left." A sad smile crossed his lips for a moment. "She told me that she would do what she wanted to do, because that's what our country allows - freedom of choice in all things, so long as it's not illegal. To tell you the truth, I brushed it off and tried to forget about it. I really did believe it wasn't something I'd have to worry about for many, many years, and I hope you'll also believe that it wasn't something I was ever considering accepting."

"But something changed," I observed, knowing that this was not how the story ended.

Sean nodded, his eyes clouding with the past. "There was a terrible, awful mistake made by someone in the prison where the man we'd arrested and convicted was placed. They let him out on day release by mistake. Lisa was murdered. This time, nothing was taken by the killer, but there was a strange symbol burned into the hardwood floor in the living room. Do you remember the oriental rug in front of the fireplace? It's beneath that." He shook his head and sighed. "Obviously, the killer never came back to prison, and we failed to find him again. He's still out there somewhere to this day, and I don't have the first idea about how to find him." He shook his head, his mouth a grim line.

"Is that why you accepted the will?" I prompted when he seemed lost to the sands of time.

"Yes and no," Sean said, looking conflicted. "I accepted it when I was summoned to the will reading. It was there that I finally found out the motive behind both crimes - the motive that Lisa Farrow had never told me she knew."

I drew in a sharp breath, my mind jumping to that symbol on the floor and the mystery surrounding all of these horrible happenings. I knew it was morbid, but I felt my pulse quicken as I scented a new puzzle to solve.

"She'd left a letter to be read out prior to the will reading that I'd been summoned to. In the letter, she claimed that the house was subject to a terrible curse. The owner of the property would be doomed to live a life with a violent end, but in return for being the guardian of the house, a great world of mysteries, success, and fulfilment in life would open up to them."

"Intriguing," I commented, still wondering how that would have changed Sean's stance. He wasn't someone who hungered for anything more than the ability to do his job and to make a difference where he could. His ambitions were simple, and besides, he wouldn't have believed in such superstitious nonsense back then.

"There was more to it than that," he continued, confirming my suspicions. "The letter also said that somewhere within the house, there's an object of great power that is responsible for the mixed blessing. She then claimed that it was this item that people were looking for when they came to rob the house. Lisa said she didn't know where it was, or how to find it, but she believed there must be a way to retrieve it." Sean sighed. "At the time, I thought she was crazy. Perhaps she'd even written this letter in a daze after the trauma of the first robbery. The next paragraph explained that she was leaving the house to me because she believed that the curse would only activate if a person had certain innate abilities that would trigger it, and she knew that I would be completely safe."

He glanced at me. "I now believe that Lisa was talking about magic. It's having magic that triggers the curse of the house… maybe." He ran a hand through his hair again. "I'm not sure at all. The letter finished by saying that - even though the item might be beyond my understanding - she hoped that with my detective skills, I might be able to locate it and also work out a way to destroy the thing. In the meantime, she suggested that I took some serious security measures and kept my guard up. Lisa's last written words to me explained that there was no one else, and that she was begging me to accept the house and the money as payment for becoming its caretaker and guardian for the good of so many people. She added that I might never understand how much was at stake, but she hoped that I would remember how sincere she'd been and take this matter as seriously as I had taken the crime that was committed against her."

He looked at me. "That was what pushed me into accepting - the knowledge that there was clearly something going on involving the property that I didn't understand, and the off chance that it might be enough to draw Lisa's killer back to try again. I think that, more than anything, pushed me into saying yes against my better judgement. Deep down, I was hoping that the killer would come back."

"And he never did?" I guessed.

"A couple of people have tried to break-in since, but I do have a fairly sophisticated security system. It works very well, so long as no one tries anything direct, like posting a voodoo doll through my front door," he said with an embarrassed smile, referencing a time when he'd overreacted massively to an unexpected delivery. "I haven't found anything that looks like an evil and powerful object during the time I've spent living in my home, but ever since I came to accept that magic is very real, the unexpected inheritance has taken on a different meaning. I've spent countless hours wondering if my knowledge and acceptance of magic is enough to bring the curse down on me."

I gave Sean the once over with witch sight. "You don't look cursed. Has anything curse-like happened to you?"

He shot me a bemused look.

I bit my lip. "Yes, I suppose there has been an uptick in crime and trouble recently," I added, thinking of everything Sean and I had been through.

The ghost of a smile passed across his lips. Our memories together were dramatic, and sometimes traumatic, but the many trials we'd been through had resulted in the formation of an unbreakable bond.

Sean cleared his throat. "I'm still not sure if Lisa Farrow was telling the truth about the house and what might be in it. I've never found any evidence to support her version of events, but I've been cautious all the same." His grey eyes found mine, his expression growing even more serious. "The reason why I've never told you any of this, or invited you to spend time at my house, isn't because I wanted to hide the fact that it was given to me in a will by a murder victim. It was because I was worried the curse would fall upon you, if you spent too much time there with me. If there is a curse, it has to fall on someone, doesn't it?" Sean asked.

I bit my lip and shot him an uncertain look. I wasn't sure about that, but it needed investigating. I considered the logic behind Sean's decision to keep me away from his house. It sounded so farfetched that I knew it had to be true, because Sean was not the sort of person who came up with colourful stories for the fun of it. In truth, I doubted he was capable of coming up with colourful anything, being so practically minded. What bothered me most about the whole thing was not that Sean had stayed silent… it was how Jesse Heathen had cherrypicked the truth and twisted it in order to make me think that Sean's secret was something shameful and malicious. And I couldn't believe that I had fallen for it. "I want to come and take a look around your house, if you'll let me."

Sean's grey eyes grew warm. "Of course. It was foolish of me to think that I was protecting you when I don't even know what I'm protecting you from."

I smiled back at him. "It's okay. I should never have let Jesse Heathen get to me."

A troubled look came into Sean's eyes. "Why do you think he wanted to drive a wedge between us? Do you think…" A slight blush came into his cheeks and he hesitated, unsure of how to say his next words. "Do you think he might be in love with you?"

I almost laughed out loud at the idea of Jesse being in love with anyone other than himself. It seemed incredibly unlikely. "If he is, then it's unrequited," I promised Sean with a jocular smile, not wanting to take any of this too seriously.

The smile slid from my face.

"Unrequited love," I repeated, my brain suddenly making several connections at once.

"What is it?" Sean looked alarmed, especially as we'd just been talking about Jesse.

"Aunt Linda's been making a love potion this morning. I walked down the stairs and recognised the ingredients by their scents - rue, peppercorns, and lemon. I bet there was some cayenne in there, too."

"It's a standard love spell!" Aunt Linda called down the stairs from where she'd definitely been listening in. "Hot and spicy, and works real quick!"

"Someone came into the apothecary and bought those ingredients really recently. It was the stand-in mayor, Anita Heron... and I think I might know who she's holding a candle for." I quickly explained the conversation we'd had on the day she'd visited my shop, and how I'd wondered why she'd made Andy's family tragedy seem like the centre of the universe, whilst speaking scathingly of Lorna. It all seemed so obvious now.

"Do you think it might be relevant to the case?" Sean asked, encouraging me to continue my theorising.

I tilted my head while I thought about it. "Initially I wondered if Anita Heron might have developed a love for the power she gained as stand-in mayor, but she makes it appear that she doesn't actually want the limelight to be focused on her at all. However, getting rid of the rivals of someone she has strong feelings for, in order for that person to succeed, could be a motive for murder."

"Do you believe that Anita's affections remain unrequited?" Sean enquired, rubbing his stubble.

"If she's trying love spells, then probably - unless she's managed to get one to work for her, but they're notoriously unreliable, especially when the target is already in a stable relationship." I pulled a face, wondering in what world someone would refer to Andy and Lorna as 'stable', but nonetheless, it seemed to work for them. "However, that doesn't necessarily mean that Andy is unaware of Anita's feelings."

"You think he might be using her?"

"Possibly. The question is… how far is she willing to go to get her man? And if Andy is using her, how far is he willing to push her to further his own political ambitions?"

13

THE GLOVES ARE FINALLY OFF

The Carats lived in the old vicarage that had since been converted into a residential property when the local church had downsized its operations in Wormwood. They retained the church itself and the hall attached to it, but these days, vicars visited Wormwood from other places, and none of them stuck around for long in our town.

The old vicarage was a beautiful building made from the local sandstone, and it must have cost a pretty penny to purchase. I remembered that Andy worked as a business consultant for a tech firm, but I wasn't sure about Lorna. Something told me she had an equally high-flying career. It didn't surprise me that the Carats' political ambitions matched their ambitions in life, which had clearly resulted in success. I found myself wondering if they ever managed to find time to sit back and enjoy it.

I was still daydreaming when we heard the shouting.

Sean shot me an alarmed look and we rushed around the side of the house, pushing open the old garden gate that separated the front from the back garden. The gate was ancient and missing a handle, so we made it inside with ease. What I saw when we exited the shrub border made me freeze with horror.

A figure dressed in black and wearing a balaclava was running across the lawn towards a group of three women. He appeared to have a large knife in his hand. All three ladies were on their feet shouting and pointing.

"They're not running. Why aren't they running?" I hissed to Sean as we rushed towards the unfolding horror.

With a strangled yell, the running man lifted the knife over his head to strike down the three mayoral candidates. I just had time to register that the knife had moved in a strange way before Rhiannon kicked him squarely in the stomach, making him double up and drop the weapon. Whilst he was still trying to catch his breath, Lorna grabbed his legs and lifted upwards, sending the hapless attacker flying through the air. He landed in a crumpled heap on the grass, which is when Jade Rey pulled a dagger out of the sheath attached to her upper thigh and held it against his throat.

"I'll take it from here!" Sean shouted, alarmed by the sight of the sharp blade.

Jade glanced at him. "I think we've got it under control," she said, not moving the blade. "Let's unmask this murderer, once and for all." With a smooth flick of her wrist, she seized the woollen balaclava and removed it from the face of the beaten man.

We all stood in contemplative silence for a moment, looking at the person responsible for so much fear and horror.

"Who the heck are you?" Jade said, speaking for all of us.

A young man with a spray of pimples across his cheeks, and dirty blonde hair that stuck up in clumps after sweating inside the balaclava, looked desperately back and forth between us all. "I… it was just supposed to be a joke! The knife's not even real. It's rubber, look!" I glanced across at the knife and realised he was telling the truth. It also accounted for the strange movement I'd observed when he'd struck. "Me and my mates heard about some maniac running around town with a knife or something, bumping off the people who want to be mayor, and we thought it would be a funny prank if we…" He trailed off, hopefully realising that pretending to be a murderer was not funny in the slightest.

"Isn't it interesting that you went after the female candidates?" Lorna said, heaping scorn on the prankster. "I suppose you thought we'd scare more easily?"

He blushed, but didn't deny it.

"How did you know that these women were going to be here?" I asked the badly behaved young man.

Lorna Carat answered for him. "I posted a photo to Instagram when my fellow candidates arrived to have a civilised discussion about the progress of our campaigns, and how alliances might be forged between us. I must have accidentally selected 'share location'. This little rat must have seen it."

The young man gulped and nodded in confirmation. Jade's knife was still pressing into his skin. Judging by the slanting smile on her face, she was rather enjoying the chance to use a weapon she'd undoubtedly made herself.

Sean walked over and handcuffed the young man to save him from the weapons expert. "I'll call the officers I have watching this house. They can take him away."

"Clearly, they're not watching closely enough," Rhiannon commented, frowning at the young man dressed in black.

Sean stayed silent, unable to argue with that judgement.

"It was really impressive watching all of you take down a man who could have genuinely been trying to harm you," I said while the police officers were entering through the garden gate. Sean led the prankster towards them, no doubt to both hand him over and deliver a dressing down to his colleagues for snoozing on the job.

"He shouldn't have assumed we were an easy target," Jade said, flipping her knife and catching it again, before sliding it back into the sheath.

"I've got a black belt in jujitsu, and I've taken a kendo exam in Japan," Rhiannon said brightly.

"I'm a competitive powerlifter," Lorna revealed, flexing a rather impressive bicep.

"And I just like sharp objects," Jade finished with a bright grin.

I nodded, silently observing that the young prankster had picked the wrong people to mess with… whilst also acknowledging that all three women here had the potential strength and skill to swing an axe to devastating effect. "Are you really here to discuss working together on your campaigns?" I asked, finding it a little surprising that there were collaborations taking place so close to the polling date.

"Of course not! We were actually planning how we're going to kill the rest of the men running for mayor before its time to cast the ballots," Jade Rey said with a wicked grin.

Rhiannon looked shocked and Lorna looked thoughtful.

"It's interesting that you can joke about something so serious," I commented.

It was Lorna who replied. "What else is there to do but laugh when all the world around you is falling apart? It's horrible that any of this has happened, but we collectively made a decision to continue with the election and not let this person scare us away, and that's what we are going to do. I can promise you that we didn't meet to discuss the demise of my husband and that other loudmouth, Jesse Heathen, but we did meet to discuss an alliance of protection and a commitment to continue our campaigns. We may be rivals, but that doesn't mean our competition extends to wanting the others to die. We were meeting to talk about looking out for each other. After all, the police haven't done a brilliant job of that so far, have they? Perhaps there's something to Jesse Heathen's suggestion after all."

"I'm always in support of extra funding for the police," Sean said, making his return and ignoring the criticism.

"Is that so?" Lorna said, shooting a skeptical look at him, before glancing back at me. Apparently, there'd been some discussion about our personal and business relations overlapping. We'd never made a secret of our relationship, but we hadn't advertised it either.

"This is getting out of hand," Rhiannon murmured, looking back in the direction of the garden gate. Her shoulders moved up and down as she fought to keep her breathing steady. "All I want to do is make the town a cleaner place. I didn't think I was going up against a psychopath with an unknown agenda. I only came here today to tell the others that I was going to pull out of the election, but they've convinced me that staying in is the right thing to do." Determination flashed in her eyes. A second later, thoughtfulness overtook her expression. "Besides… so far, it seems as though the killer has justified what they're doing, or warned us prior to an attack. We've all decided to be as open and honest about our pasts as we can. It might be enough to keep us all safe."

"Well, I think this might be the end of our meeting, ladies," Lorna said, reading the expressions on our faces.

We walked into the house through the back door as a group, Sean and I hovering in the hallway whilst Lorna wished goodbye to the other candidates. She shut the door behind them, bending down to pick up a brown recycled envelope that was on the doormat, where it had fallen from the letterbox. "What can I do for you?" she asked, a lot of the prickliness disappearing now that we were alone. I inwardly raised my eyebrows, wondering if Lorna wore a personality when she was out in public and tried on a different one at home. I also wondered if she had a third character she liked to play. One that liked to get choppy with an axe.

"We're actually here to see Andy," Sean explained, our visit having been somewhat derailed thus far. Prior to coming to the Carats' house, we'd agreed that we should begin our search for the truth with Andy rather than Anita - in order to find out how much he knew and whether Anita had tried to use a love spell on him yet.

Lorna opened the envelope and withdrew the letter inside. "He'll be lurking in his office upstairs. Ever since the library incident, he's been in there sulking as much as he can. He hasn't told me anything more than the statement you wrote for him, claiming that you asked him to stay silent about the details. I know my husband. If he's silent about anything, it's because he's embarrassed about it. I'm guessing he wasn't exactly the hero of the hour." She raised her eyebrows at us.

We didn't say anything, but the lack of response seemed to be confirmation enough for her.

"Typical male ego. I'm sure however he behaved was just human nature, but no, he can't confess to being a coward because he thinks it will ruin his 'Mr Cool' image. He's putting pressure on himself that isn't even there. I think Wormwood's voters would appreciate a human being more than an action hero." She hesitated with the letter in her hand. "Or maybe a cat. Anyway… you can find Andy by going up the stairs and taking the first door on the left." She raised her eyebrows for a second in what I recognised as a 'good luck with that' type gesture, before she walked back through the house towards the kitchen, frowning at the letter in her hand.

We made our way up the stairs and knocked on the door we'd been directed to. "Go away!" a voice came from within, reminding me of a teenager telling a parent to leave them alone.

"Andy, it's DCI Sean Admiral and Hazel Salem here to see you about…"

"…an exclusive interview," I improvised, deciding that flat out asking him if anyone had targeted him with a love spell recently, or if he'd persuaded someone to murder people to help his campaign, probably wasn't the way to get a straight and honest answer. Sean nodded to show his approval of the new plan.

"Interview? I gave my statement about what happened in the library. Go away."

"Hazel is writing up a press release about what happened that night, and she'd like to share how instrumental you were in helping the police to put together a timeline of the crime, which could well prove crucial to solving this case. She also thought it might be a chance to share some of the things you stand for, too… in the election."

I threw an impressed look at Sean. He'd taken what I'd started and run with it.

"A press release stating that my input was crucial? Would you let me sign off on it prior to publication?" Andy asked, opening the door a crack and peering out. His previously luxuriant, golden-brown hair was standing up all over the place, but his eyes seemed bright and ready - probably at the prospect of scoring some political points. "Come on in," Andy said, pushing the door wide. His public-facing smile was back on his face and the sulky teenager act of a few moments before appeared to have been forgotten.

Sean asked Andy to recap some of the events that had taken place at the library, and I scribbled down some notes that I was going to have to shoehorn into an unplanned article later.

"How did that sound? Can you say that I took shelter only because there was no way to defend myself, and I was taking a non-violent approach? I would have confronted the killer and asked them to explain themselves and surrender, had I been armed. I'm not too shabby at self defence, but an axe is a bit much to handle, even for someone like me. Working with axes teaches you to respect them and understand the damage they can do, but they should never be abused in this way," He smiled again and glanced at my notebook. "Make sure you get that as a quote."

"Of course," I said with a smile of my own, flicking the notebook shut. "Have you spoken to Anita Heron recently? She told us she's been doing welfare checks on candidates to make sure no one is suffering from anxiety."

Andy chuckled. "She's checking to see if *we're* anxious? Anita's always been a jittery one. Did you know, she took up knife throwing, of all things, to try to calm her nerves? She was tutored by a circus performer, I believe. We chatted about it before the candidate announcement event began. She seemed to know about my wood-chopping skills." He looked thoughtful for a moment before continuing. "The interview part is finished, isn't it? Poor old Anita. She should never have been stand-in mayor, but I don't think they could persuade anyone else to take the job. She seems like a nice person. I enjoyed meeting her." He looked back and forth between us, wondering if that was what we'd wanted to hear.

"Weren't you in the same year at secondary school? I believe you were at Witchwood Community College together," I said, picking up on Andy claiming how nice it was to have met Anita, as if it had been for the first time.

Andy looked astonished. "Did we? I had no idea. I suppose she was one of the quiet ones." He shrugged. "All of that feels like such a long time ago. I'd definitely struggle to put names to faces for a lot of my school year. I didn't have any room for distraction back then. In sixth form, I won myself the scholarship to university that was handed out yearly to the fortunate student who managed to land themselves the role of student council president." He flashed a white smile. "I thought this would be a walk in the park compared to that election," he said with a laugh, before sobering immediately afterwards when he recalled how serious the current election had become. "I've won various elected positions within businesses after that, landed every promotion I've ever looked at, and now I find myself wanting to give something back to the town that welcomed me and Lorna into the fold."

I exchanged a look with Sean. It certainly didn't appear that Anita's feelings were reciprocated, or even acknowledged by the leading candidate. In fact, he barely seemed to be aware of her existence.

"Is Anita under some sort of suspicion?" Andy suddenly asked, misreading the look I'd exchanged with Sean. "I don't know her well at all, but she's been very generous by helping me with my campaign - in spite of me warning her that some might see it as biased behaviour. She even gave me a present." He indicated a small, stuffed bear that appeared to be holding a plush four-leaf clover. "I'm glad to hear that she's been doing the same for everyone. I wouldn't want to be singled out,"

"Yes, exactly," Sean lied. "Thanks for your help, Andy."

"No problem," he replied, but his expression remained thoughtful when we walked back to the door of his study. "You know, this might sound crazy, but my wife mentioned that she thought the stand-in mayor might have the hots for me. I feel rather embarrassed to even be sharing it with you. It's probably just Lorna pulling my leg. I mean, Lorna even suggested that Anita might be the one behind all of the murders, because she's gone power mad and can't bear to lose her new mayoral privileges."

Sean raised an eyebrow. "There are certainly less violent ways to delay an election, if she'd wanted to do that. Don't you think she would have tried those methods first?"

Andy nodded. "Sure, but perhaps she really does believe in her ideals and thinks that some people aren't worthy to be the mayor of this town. It could have become a passion for her - protecting a job that she's started to believe is sacred." He shrugged. "I'm probably waffling. You're the crime experts."

"Do you really believe someone would kill other people, just to become, or remain, the Mayor of Wormwood?" I asked Andy, wondering if he really took the theory he'd shared seriously. It seemed irrational when the job was not power over everyone and everything that happened in Wormwood - as much as the previous mayor had tried to make it that way and more. It was a job that was supposed to bring about good things for the town and make it a better place to live. It was an often thankless role that definitely didn't have the same allure of power as the national government.

"Different things matter different amounts to different people. You would have to ask the killer for their thoughts, but sometimes ambition makes people do things they had no idea they were even capable of doing. It's important to have big goals in life," Andy finished, looking out of the window at the blue sky beyond.

While he was momentarily distracted, I crab-walked across the office and shoved something down the back of my trousers.

"Thank you for your time, Mr Carat," Sean said when it seemed as though the mayoral candidate didn't have anything more to share.

He waited until we were back outside the old vicarage, before asking: "What did you steal?"

I pulled the 'lucky bear' out from the back of my trousers and showed it to him. Its caramel coloured fur and dopey glass eyes looked placidly back at us. I pulled the stuffed four leaf clover on the front of the bear forward enough to reveal the stitching that had been added on the rear side. It was sloppily done, which made it simple to find a loose thread and pull to make the whole thing come undone. My fingers deftly pulled out dried rue and lemon slices. Peppercorns and bright red cayenne pepper scattered over the floor, before I found two locks of hair - one mousey and one golden-brown - bound together with red string. "I stole Anita Heron's love spell."

14

UNLUCKY IN LOVE

"Thank goodness you're here," Anita Heron greeted us when we were shown up to her office in the town hall. "I haven't been able to think straight since I was told what happened to Graham Jinx. I felt like a zombie through the debate the other day. I've told everyone who will listen that we should just cancel the election until all of this can be worked out, and the person responsible found and punished, but everyone ignores me." She wrung her hands. "Everyone always ignores me."

"How have you found being the stand-in mayor?" I asked, smiling encouragingly at the other woman.

"Oh, you know. All work and no play. It's been a good challenge. I'm almost sorry to give it up," Anita confessed, pushing her red-winged glasses up her nose and looking around the interior of the office of the mayor, which was wood panelled and featured some rather lovely bookcases. It was the sort of place that spoke of history and prestige, and I could imagine that it might become a hard place to leave.

"You never thought about running for election yourself?" I asked, wanting to check where her ambitions lay.

She smiled and shook her head, almost laughing at the idea. "No, it's been good taking on this role, but I'm not the sort of person who wins elections that make a real difference - like being mayor, or something important like that. People vote for charisma, great policies, and someone that they can see taking the town into a new era as a leader. I've never been called a leader in my life," she said with a sorry smile. "But, not everyone is born to be that. I'm good at what I do, working behind the scenes, and that's the way it should be. Being on the town council was my way of doing that. It's been lovely to have the opportunity to help others when I can. I also volunteer teaching I.T. to our older residents, who need to get online in this modern age but aren't sure how. I used to be quite the computer whizz, but that probably goes without saying when you look at the rest of my personality." She bobbed her page-boy haircut back and forth. "The classic computer-obsessed recluse!"

She cleared her throat and looked awkward when neither of us spoke. "You know… I've heard a few rumours that I might have had something to do with the deaths because I've gone mad with power, but I can't stress enough how ridiculous that is. It was even said to my face when I dared to suggest that we postpone the election for safety reasons." She shook her head. "If I'd gone mad with power, don't you think I'd have done something more dramatic to make my mark? Don't you think I would have run for mayor myself and done whatever it took to hold onto this position? Hoping that an election will be postponed indefinitely is ridiculous, and as for leaving a mark, all I've done is keep things ticking over as a caretaker should. You can have all of the reports on that to check, if you want. I've got nothing to hide, regarding what I've done here. You won't find it very gripping, but I think I've done a pretty decent job… one I should be thanked for doing rather than vilified!" There was heat in her voice when she finished and colour flushed into her cheeks. "That's why you've really come here, isn't it? That's why you're asking about what I think of the job, and why I'm not running for election. You've come to call me power hungry, just like the rest of them!"

"Not at all," Sean said, recovering quickly. "You were right when you greeted us - we're here to talk about what happened to Graham Jinx and find out how the election plans are progressing. We also thought you might be able to give us some more insight into the candidates. As someone who is overseeing this process, you're better placed to make judgements than those who are involved in the race itself. We would greatly value your opinion. Have you got a favourite for mayor? Someone you think is best suited to the role?"

"Oh, well… I suppose I'm a voter, too!" she said, the red flush receding. She patted her hair absentmindedly. "I think that Andy Carat would do a very good job. He has all of the charisma of our last mayor - perhaps even more - except he seems more levelheaded."

That wouldn't be difficult, I thought, remembering the last mayor's plot to take over the world.

"What about his wife, Lorna? She seems to be very capable and accomplished," I said, knowing I was putting the cat amongst the pigeons.

"Well, uh, yes, she *has* got a lot of life experience," Anita said, making it sound like it was a bad thing. "However, I can't help but wonder if she doesn't want it too much. I worry that…" she frowned down at the floor, before risking a look up from beneath her eyelashes to see how her dramatic turn was working out "…I worry that she might be the one who's taken it too far. She's very competitive, you know. I remember that from our school days. If she realised her husband was gaining more support than her, who knows what she might've done?"

"If that were true, wouldn't she have done away with her husband first?" I pointed out, not exactly buying into Anita's act.

"Well, I'm not saying it's *definitely* her. It could be that other woman, Jade. She makes weapons for films. Given what we know about the current crime spree, she should be your prime suspect, shouldn't she?"

"Jade Rey has a rather convincing alibi," Sean said.

"People lie," Anita countered.

"We were with her when the incident at the library occurred, and we'd been with her for a long time prior to that. She may be good at forging weapons, but I don't think she can be in two places at the same time."

That stumped Anita. "That environmental woman, Rhiannon, she's… too quiet. They always say it's the quiet ones you have to watch out for, don't they?"

It was at that moment that Sean's phone rang.

"Hello? You've received a threat? Stay calm. We will be with you as quickly as possible," he said, before hanging up.

He shot an unhappy look in Anita's direction, unsatisfied that we hadn't managed to get to the bottom of her motives involving Andy. "We have to go. Thank you for your time."

We left Anita Heron in her borrowed office, undoubtedly still wondering what the purpose of our visit had really been.

* * *

"Timing is everything!" Sean complained when we were

driving across town. "All of the surveillance teams have been recalled to be dressed down by the local area chief for not doing their jobs properly. Now I'll be the one who's in trouble for not doing *my* job properly."

"You're doing your best," I reassured him, but even to my ears, the words sounded limp.

"Those background checkers also need to be struck off. I've read through all of the files they put together since this started, and there was nothing about Anita Heron's knife throwing skills, Andy Carat's woodchopping prowess, Rhiannon's martial arts abilities, or Lorna's powerlifting pastime." He shook his head. "I suppose people in a job like that have a list of facts to find and places to dig, in order to find them, and never think outside of the box, even though outside of the box is where most things seem to take place."

I nodded, letting Sean have his rant. Sometimes, you needed to speak your frustrations out loud in order to be able to focus again.

Rhiannon opened the periwinkle blue door of her bungalow and strode down the path when she saw the car pull up on the street outside. "I didn't see who delivered it. I was in the kitchen and I heard the letterbox open and shut, which I thought was strange because the post lady had already been. This was what they delivered," she said, holding out a brown envelope. "I'd already touched it all over by the time I realised it might be evidence, sorry."

"That's no problem at all," Sean said, stepping right back into his role as a professional after voicing his frustrations. He took the envelope and removed the letter inside, his eyes scanning the page. "Organise and attend a vigil tomorrow for the candidates who didn't make it to election night. When you are there, reveal your sins. I know you aren't the person you're pretending to be,

Rhiannon Garda. Defy me, and you will be the third," he read out loud.

Rhiannon gulped and fiddled with a strand of her dark hair, her eyes focusing on the horizon as she fought to hold herself steady.

"Do you know what the writer means?" I asked, as gently as I could.

"Yes, I have to organise some sort of vigil," the other woman said, looking horrified by the prospect of having to put together an event at such short notice.

"What about the accusation that you aren't the person you're pretending to be?" I tried again.

Rhiannon's eyes flickered back and forth, like a cornered rabbit. "It, uh, it means…" She cleared her throat. "I'm not very good at being environmentally friendly. In fact, I've done some pretty terrible things to the environment," she confessed, looking shamefaced. "That's why I'm running as the green candidate for Wormwood, I wanted to change my ways and offset some of the things I've done in the past, but if I'd told anyone the truth, no one would vote for me! I'm a total hypocrite!"

"What did you do?" Sean asked, apparently as curious as I was about what one woman could possibly have done to make herself, and the killer, believe that she was a walking environmental disaster.

Rhiannon wrung her hands. "I'm a computer programmer. A good one. I've done work in the past for many different companies, and while I tried to only work with those I thought were doing good work, the money the others offered was… tempting. And then I justified it to myself by saying that I wasn't the one personally polluting the environment when I worked for the single-use plastic businesses. But now… now I can see how that looks. I'll come clean about it at this vigil. Then it's done, isn't it? I'll be safe." She exhaled. "Staying alive is more important than becoming mayor."

"Those shouldn't be your only options," I commented, inwardly furious that someone had given themselves the right to cause anyone else to think this way.

"Can you think of anyone who might be likely to send you this type of threat - anyone who might know about your work with environmentally unfriendly companies?" Sean asked, scenting the chance for a breakthrough.

Rhiannon frowned while she considered. "I'm not sure. I don't share anything publicly about my work, because a lot of what I do involves security, and if hackers figure out who the programmer was, well… it makes it easier for them. Everyone has their own style and their own flaws," she said, undoubtedly dumbing it down for us. "I've worked with Andy Carat before. Not directly, but he was the consultant at an information technology firm who contracted me for a job. She shook her head. "I don't know if he could have found out anything from that by somehow getting hold of my work record, or why he would even want to. Although, I did hear a couple of things about him when I worked that job. Someone mentioned that he'd just been promoted, but they didn't like his methods of getting the promotion. I'm afraid it wasn't anything more specific than that, but the person I overheard when I was working at their headquarters called Andy a nasty piece of work." She glanced between us. "I haven't actually thought about it again until right this second. It probably isn't relevant," she added, backtracking.

There was a muffled meow from down by my feet.

"Is that the cat that's running for mayor?" Rhiannon asked, looking curiously at the black cat who'd arrived on her doorstep.

"No, this is his far more mayor-appropriate brother," I

said, bending down and accepting the item that Hedge had been carrying in his mouth. It was sticky but still legible.

I've received a threat. A really threatening threat. Come to my place right now. It's urgent.

- Jesse Heathen, future Mayor of Wormwood

Not so threatening that he was too scared to add that signature, I thought, unimpressed. The only thing that made me think it was urgent or serious in the slightest was that Hedge had been dispatched. Jesse knew mobile phone reception was questionable in Wormwood, so he'd used his familiar to make sure I got the message.

"We have to go," I said to Sean, before turning back to Rhiannon Garda. "Thank you for reporting the threat you received. DCI Admiral will make sure it's properly investigated and the surveillance officers will be returning imminently. In the meantime..." I considered the display she'd put on earlier today "...keep fighting the good fight."

"Has something happened?" she asked.

"No," I said, willing it to be true. "We're going to stop it before it happens. No one else is going to die."

I should have learnt to keep bold statements like that to myself.

15

THE SNAKE AT THE END OF THE WORLD

The building at the end of a lane that led to nowhere, just off the main high-street, looked every bit as gloomy as I remembered it. The flat with a shop beneath it had previously been leased to a man named Hellion Grey. He'd met an unfortunate end and the un-squeamish Jesse had scented an opportunity and had taken on the premises himself.

The shop window was dark when we approached. Someone had painted the glass black on the inside. I glanced at Sean, who looked less than thrilled to be rushing to Jesse's aid. Then, my eyes went down to Hedge, who'd ridden back with us in the car. The yellow-eyed cat didn't look any more impressed than Sean. I wondered if this was all a wild goose chase and Jesse was playing another of his games.

Muttering under my breath, I gave the front door a frustrated shove and walked inside the defunct shop.

The burning arrows that shot towards me like a deadly rain of fire were not the welcome I'd anticipated.

I was only just quick enough.

The arrows thunked into the shield I'd whipped out of the in-between faster than my brain could follow. For a second, I was too shocked to do anything. Then the rage kicked in. "Regular arrows aren't good enough for you? You had to light them on fire, too?" I yelled into the dim interior of the shop. The place had a musty smell to it, like no doors or windows had been opened for a while and it had been quite some time since someone had lived here. It was strange if Jesse was staying in Wormwood, but perhaps he hadn't got round to cleaning yet.

"Hazel? Is that really you?" a voice called out from somewhere upstairs. It sounded odd - smaller and further away than it should have done. It was like someone shouting out of a goldfish bowl.

"No, it's a crazed axe murderer," I yelled back, seriously unhappy about the arrows. Deep down, I was most annoyed with myself for not checking the door prior to opening it, but to be fair, I hadn't expected Jesse to be concerned enough to boobytrap his own house. Right from the very start, he'd claimed that he doubted the killer would bother going after him - even though he had a history shady enough to make even a professional politician blush. I wondered what had changed.

"In that case, please go away," Jesse replied, but he sounded happier already. "Be careful where you step when you come up here. The stairs are a bit... sharp."

"Threatening threat indeed," I muttered as I squinted at the stairs in an attempt to predict what, exactly, Jesse had done to turn them into a deathtrap. "I'm the one who's going to be a threatening threat when I find the little devil!" I glanced back at Hedge. "Didn't feel like warning me?"

Hedge stuck his nose in the air and went to lie down in

a very plush looking tartan basket. Apparently he'd done his job and nothing above and beyond that.

"So ungrateful," I muttered, thinking of when I'd taken him in as a kitten. Kids were never grateful.

The stairs were laced with so much spell work I could barely see the wood they were made from. With a frown, I reached out to touch one of the spells. There was a small explosion as a hundred small missiles and traps sprung, one after the other - each triggered by the movement of the next. When the sawdust settled and all was quiet once more, the stairs had been remodelled, and not in a way that any conventional interior designer would approve of. Splinters stuck up in the air and unusual pointy items now studded the banister, from ninja stars to crab forks. I shook my head and walked up the stairs. Jesse might be doing a pretty good impression of being paranoid, but he really needed to think his traps through. All of those spells, and a single poke had been all it had taken to set the lot off.

"Don't give him advice on how to do it better," Sean said, apparently reading my mind. He pushed the magic-seeing glasses he'd been gifted by my father further up his nose as he surveyed the damage.

Once we made it to the top of the stairs, I dismantled a few more traps. "Jesse?" I called out as we passed a startling array of charms, from lucky clovers to horseshoes and rabbits' feet. There were other things, too - amulets of protection from all different cultures dangled from the ceiling, like Jesse was living in the middle of a giant trinket shop. I glanced down at the floor and noted the grey powder that had been placed across the threshold of the room all of the items seemed to be leading us to. Graveyard dust mixed with salt - another protection method passed down through generations.

This time, I knocked on the door.

"Come in, there aren't any other traps," Jesse's voice came from inside the room. It still sounded strange. When I pushed open the door, I found out why. Jesse had constructed a spell around himself that was bright with blue light. The orb was acting like a bubble to keep Jesse protected from any and all attacks. Attacks that he apparently had reason to believe might be imminent.

"Why are you hiding in a blue ball of light?" Sean asked.

Jesse blinked. "What's happening? How does he know that? Ah, the glasses." The devil had decent powers of observation. "One of James Monroe's inventions, I presume? That could be interesting. It could open up a whole new market of people who don't have magic, but can see it, and would undoubtedly want to gain it for themselves using any means possible."

"Don't even think about making any deals again," I warned him. "Besides, no one but Sean is getting a pair of glasses. It would change everything, and not for the better."

"For a moment there, I almost forgot about my terrible predicament," Jesse said, the excitement dying in his eyes. "Now it's all come back to me. I'm doomed. Totally doomed."

I exchanged a look with Sean. Neither of us was particularly inclined to take Jesse seriously, especially when he was so good at making people dance to his tune.

"What sort of threat did you receive?" Sean asked, not even getting out his notepad.

"It's there in the envelope on the table beneath the mirror," Jesse said, nodding towards a small dressing table beneath something covered in cloth. "Mirrors can be gateways," he explained. "You never know what's on the other side of a mirror."

"A girl named Alice?" Sean suggested.

"Look who brought his sense of humour along today!"

Jesse said, his forehead creasing. "Ho ho ho, I don't need to take my police duties seriously because the person in trouble happens to be a god. That's discrimination! I deserve the same protection as the rest of the candidates. Having said that, your protection of them thus far has not been very successful. I want *better* protection than the rest of the candidates."

While this was going on, I'd made it to the table and opened up the envelope. A quick glance told me that it was the same type as the one Rhiannon had handed us before we'd come here.

Jesse Heathen
You are a snake. The best way to deal with a snake is to find a bigger snake to consume it. I think you know which snake I'll be sending after you.
You'd better start running.

The letter finished with a hand-drawn sigil. I tilted the paper back and forth, but the swirling lines and runes didn't mean anything in particular to me.

"It's the sigil of the Midgard Serpent," Jesse said when he saw me looking blank. "Learn some history!"

"Isn't that exactly what the Serpent is… history? It's tied in with your end of the world mythology, isn't it?"

Jesse made high-pitched mimicking sounds. "Of course it is! Why don't you know any of this? Have you no interest in where I come from? Honestly, any normal human would have pored over my past, hoping to seek some divine favour from me. This is so tiresome."

"Did it happen?" Sean asked, looking genuinely curious.

"The end of the world? Yes, of course it did. It will happen again some day soon, no doubt. Every belief system has its day. Plus, things always go in cycles. They always have done and always will do - ending and beginning again and again."

"So, why are you afraid of a snake? Hasn't the worst already happened? Doesn't it no longer exist?" Sean asked, looking sheepish as he said it.

"Well, well... I didn't expect you to be the one to have done your homework,"Jesse said, looking semi-impressed. "You're both wrong and right. The Midgard Serpent isn't sunning itself in the Seychelles, but it also doesn't exactly *not* exist anymore. The nature of my kind's existence is rather complicated, but the gist of it is, it's possible to come back from almost not existing to being in this world again if certain things happen. After all, I'm proof enough of that." He patted his chest, demonstrating that he was definitely solid. "Many of my brethren figured it out, too. Some were also helped back into this world to return to causing petty mischief and await a time when they might rise to greatness again." He snorted. "Total nonsense. I've told them all to enjoy life for what it is and find another occupation, but no one listens to the trickster."

"I can't imagine why," I commented.

Jesse rolled his eyes, as if I were the one who was talking nonsense. "The point is, the writer of this threat definitely knows something about me and about everything I've just said, and I do not want to have to deal with that snake again. I spent long enough, an eternity in fact, in its company... and that's more than enough. I don't need some small town psycho digging up the past."

"That's what happens when you get into politics. People dig up the past," Sean said - probably a little too smugly.

Jesse noticed and glared at him. "Less of the holier than

thou attitude and more of the finding and stopping this maniac, before they conduct any rituals that might set something loose in the land that should not ever be set loose again. Trust me, it won't just be my problem."

"We'll sort it," I said with a surprising amount of certainty.

"You will?" Jesse said, the wind taken out of his sails.

"It's our number one priority."

He squinted at me through his blue cocoon, trying to detect any trace of sarcasm. "Oh. Well, in that case… that's all I wanted. You'll tell me when you've got them, won't you? I've got Hecate out guarding the perimeter, just in case anything tries to sneak up on me," he said, referring to his hellhound.

"That sounds sensible. You should wait here and we will stay in touch."

"What about a panic button?" Jesse said, looking uncertain again.

"A what?" Sean ground out.

"A panic button. It's a thing you give people in danger, and when they push it, you're alerted and come running immediately," Jesse said, like he was explaining it to a very small child.

"You really think something like that would work in Wormwood with our history of technology problems?" I countered. Part of the reason why Wormwood had remained a small and relatively affordable town, in spite of its favourable location in the South East of England, was because modern technology was unreliable at best in the area.

"Well, obviously with some magical enhancement," Jesse replied. "I bet you could pull one out of the in-between right now." He paused expectantly.

Just to show some sort of willing, I stuck my hand into

the place between dimensions that supplied an appropriate item for whatever the current dangerous situation was. When I looked at what I'd pulled out, I was annoyed to discover a small red button on a string and what looked like a pager that would receive the signal, should there be anything to panic about. "I wasn't serious!" I muttered to the in-between, ticked off that it was choosing now to supply the exact thing Jesse had requested when I almost never got exactly what I wanted.

Jesse cradled the button like it was the most precious gem in the world. "Help me, Hazel. You're my only hope."

"You're definitely mayor material... always making other people solve your problems for you," Sean said, looking deeply unimpressed with the behaviour of the aspiring mayor, who'd claimed he was so powerful that no mortal killer would dare try to do anything to him. It just went to show, this killer was excellent at working out people's weaknesses and getting a reaction out of them.

I wondered if they were also playing on the weaknesses of those who were trying to solve their terrible crimes.

16

CURIOUSER AND CURIOUSER

We were driving back through town when Sean's phone got enough signal to ring. He pulled over to the side of the road and got out of the car before he answered. I got out, too, and watched as he began to pace back and forth, indicating that it was probably going to be a fairly long conversation.

I discovered we were standing outside Wormwood's version of a town museum. The Wormwood Curio Centre and Shoppe was a narrow building sandwiched between a tarot card reader and a shoe repair shop, that was advertising a special price for the repair of any ruby slippers that customers might bring in - no questions asked. The front windows of the almost-museum looked like they could do with a good clean. It was only just possible to see the frames of the photographs that must have been put on display a very long time ago, as they were almost completely faded by the sun. A suit of armour took pride of place at the centre of the window. Instead of a sword, the knight was clutching a pink polka dot decorated umbrella, which bore a label saying that it had been used to get to safety by a local witch during a storm back in the eighties. It didn't specify whether she'd used it as a boat, or à la Mary Poppins, but perhaps the owner of the shop had wanted to keep people guessing.

Or perhaps the umbrella was just an umbrella that they'd picked up at a boot fair and labelled.

I glanced over at Sean, but he was still deep in conversation. Clearly, the call was about something important. On a whim, I checked my pockets and found I had the pound coin it cost to enter the curio part of the shop. With nothing better to do, I pushed open the grimy door and stepped into Wormwood's world of yesteryear.

There was a dull clank when I placed my entrance fee into the honesty box by the door. Nothing moved inside the building, so I assumed that the proprietor was probably on their lunch break. I'd visited before. It had once been a cool place to come with teenage friends to see who got creeped out by the taxidermy exhibits and the weird waxwork figures. That was a long time ago now, but on first inspection, it appeared as if nothing had changed since my last visit.

I didn't know what changes I'd been expecting. History had a habit of remaining constant.

I stuck my hands in my pockets and wandered further inside. A sign thick with red, drippy paint, that was supposed to look like blood, read 'Chamber of Horrors', pointing the way down a narrow hallway. I remembered this exhibition being the main reason why teenagers had been so interested in coming here. It had almost been a rite of passage to scare your friends by moving the exhibits and pretending they'd come alive. Naturally, the owner had had something to say about that.

I looked around, wondering if Mr Hammond was still in charge. I thought he might well be. History remained constant, but people often did, too, sticking to the habits they had formed over the years. This place was one big, unchanged habit.

I walked down the corridor, looking at the photos on the walls that I'd certainly never bothered with when I'd been younger. Photos were boring things that you had to endure whenever someone you knew went on holiday and returned with an album stuffed full of them. My past visits had been all about the weird and wonderful things you could see and touch, not the stories and images behind them.

I paused by a board called 'Local Unsolved Mysteries'. When I'd returned to Wormwood to launch my local interest magazine, *Tales From Wormwood*, I'd published a few of these 'unsolved mysteries' myself, telling ghost stories about headless horsemen in Wormwood Forest and other tall tales. I hadn't known the difference between what was real magical influence and what was pure fabrication for tourists back then, but the same stories were listed here. The smile faded from my face when I read about an arson attack on an orphanage one hundred years ago in Hobbling that had never been solved. Perhaps there'd been no local crime fighting duo back then. No one to put the pieces together.

There were more recent stories, too, cut from local newspapers. My eyes scanned a story about a hit and run. Jim Garda had tragically been hit by a car and killed aged eighteen when walking across a zebra crossing. The driver had fled the scene and there'd been no witnesses to the accident. A few flakes of red paint were all that had been left behind. Jim had been described by his family and friends as an intelligent young man, who was liked by everyone, with a bright future in leadership, taken away far too soon. *Poor Rhiannon,* I thought, remembering Anita telling me about her brother's death. It must have been terrible for her to lose her brother at such a young age and in such a violent manner.

The article next to it caught my eye. An image of Sean's house was accompanied by the headline: *Escaped Convict Returns To Murder His Last Victim*. I bit my tongue as I read the scathing text, which heaped scorn on the investigating officers and queried how such a mistake could have been made, and after it had been made, why had the now deceased woman not been informed immediately? I could see why Sean was in turmoil to this day over what had transpired. Worse still, the journalist must have done some investigating of their own because they'd continued the article by mentioning Sean by name and heavily hinting that he'd benefited directly from the murder... with rumours suggesting that he'd been the sole benefactor of the deceased's estate.

I shut my eyes, knowing how that looked and sounded. Sean had known it, too, which is why he hadn't wanted to accept the will. *And it was right here all along*, I thought, tilting my head at the newspaper clipping, which finished with the words: 'And to this day, the killer has not been caught'. It had been written in such a way that it implied that the reason the killer had never been caught was because of Sean, and that some sort of deal had been struck between him and the wanted criminal.

"Nonsense," I said, glaring at the board of unsolved mysteries and wondering if I dared to remove the blatant smear article. I hoped that every person who visited this place knew better than to believe everything that was written by the media, but without an alternative viewpoint available to read, it was easy to see how many would take it at face value.

"That was the result of the autopsy of both victims," Sean said, walking into the shop. I glanced at the honesty box and fumbled in my pocket for a second pound coin. Sean was too distracted to notice the box or the newspaper article I was subtly trying to block with my body.

"The pathologist has confirmed that the cause of death in both cases was due to decapitation. She also agrees that the weapon was almost certainly wielded by someone with a degree of skill and either strength, or knowledge of how best to utilise a weapon, so that it does most of the heavy lifting. Here's where it gets more interesting. After examining the wounds, especially those inflicted on Graham Jinx, the pathologist agrees with Andy Carat's hypothesis that the weapon used is not a sword, or a machete, but an axe. Apparently, axes tend to twist slightly upon impact, instead of making a clean cut - often crushing the vertebra rather than cutting through it neatly. She found several signs of this twisting motion and believes the fatal wounds were inflicted by a large axe."

"Like the sort of weapon Jade Rey would make for films and television?" I asked, wondering if there was something we'd missed, some way for her still to be involved in a case that seemed to have her skillset written all over it.

"Not exactly," Sean replied. "Jade makes weapons that only look like they came straight from history. This axe actually does. There was rust in the cuts to the necks and small fragments of metal that must have broken off, due to weaknesses caused by age, or faults in the original forging. The metal was tested and it turns out that the axe that was used is hundreds of years old."

"Did the pathologist find anything else?"

Sean rubbed the back of his neck. "No fingerprint or DNA residue, but she did have a theory about the differences between the two deaths. Ed Brindle was probably close to the ground when he was killed, potentially bending down to look at the silver coins we found scattered at the scene of his death. Graham Jinx was sitting in a chair, which made his decapitation harder for the murderer."

"Just like Andy said," I said, remembering how he'd been the one to theorise that the weapon used was an axe.

"Indeed," Sean agreed with the pause for consideration it deserved. "So, what we are looking for is someone who's managed to get their hands on a genuine antique weapon that they've sharpened and put to use. Where we're going to find something like that is anyone's guess. Perhaps there have been some antiques sold off at a local auction recently."

"I think I might have an idea about that," I said, glancing back at the Chamber of Horrors sign.

"Ah! Visitors!" a man greeted us, popping up from behind a dusty desk. "Welcome to the Wormwood Curio Centre and Shoppe. Is there anything in particular I can help you with today, or are you just browsing our historical exhibits?" He glanced towards the honesty box when he said it and I felt very glad that I'd already paid for the pair of us. "Don't forget to sign your name in the guestbook. We're dedicated to history here, so we love to know just who has passed through these rooms of intrigue. It's also nice to read the comments," He added with a smile that featured a gold tooth. I remembered him from the last time I'd visited this place. I'd been right to think that Mr Hammond was still the custodian of all of this history.

"We're looking for an axe. A rather large one. Have you ever sold anything like that?" I asked.

The man's bushy white eyebrows shot up. "We don't sell weapons here. It's mostly souvenirs - you know, the tat that tourists like - and occasionally a few local documents or photographs that people fancy on their walls. Family history and the like."

I shrugged at Sean. "It was worth asking," I said apologetically.

"However... there *was* a recent theft," the owner continued, like he was telling the story to a group of tourists who'd asked for a tale from times gone by, told at approximately the same pace as the original events had occurred.

"Was a really large axe stolen?" I asked, hoping we could skip the 'it was a dark and stormy night' stuff and get straight to finding out if we were barking up the right tree.

"Indeed! A very singular axe was spirited away. You may have noticed the Chamber of Horrors exhibit. The star of the show is a miniature model of a guillotine. Standing next to it, a wax model of an executioner holds an original executioner's axe from the 1700s. It gets quite the reaction from our visitors!"

"Probably because guillotines were never used in England. Only an English version called the gibbet was utilised in some areas," Sean muttered under his breath.

"It was very distressing to lose such an important item," Mr Hammond continued, pretending he hadn't heard Sean. "I often leave the shop unattended whilst I make myself meals, or take bathroom breaks. I assumed some local teenagers must have come in and taken it for some hijinks. I thought it would probably turn up again sooner or later when they got bored with it. It's a clunky old thing with a very blunt edge. I thought of it as an ornament, rather than a weapon, so I never made a fuss. Things have been taken from here before, but they inevitably turn up again." He paused and glanced up at the wall above the shop door. I followed his gaze and saw a silvery haze of magic that was undoubtedly some sort of anti-theft spell. I was certain that any thieves would discover that their consciences were pricked in an alarmingly spiky way and found themselves returning what they'd taken. It might have worked for unruly teenagers, but the killer at large had demonstrated they possessed more than enough willpower to overcome a simple charm like that.

"Why haven't you reported it to the police? Didn't you see the two recent murders by decapitation in the local papers?" Sean asked, practically spitting with rage.

Mr Hammond seemed completely oblivious to the powder keg he'd just ignited. "Well, I'd stopped thinking about the axe by then, and the papers never said exactly what had happened to those people - just that they'd lost their heads. There are many methods that will achieve the same result. I show off a lot of them in the Chamber of Horrors," he said, unable to resist another opportunity for promotion. "Anyway, since the axe didn't turn up, I've turned my attention to acquiring something else. Preferably something with more local history. I bought the axe at a random online auction for a tiny amount of money. It was a rusted old heap of junk that I cleaned up a bit, painted with some fake blood, and put on display. I've no idea where it originated from. It may never have been used in any executions at all. I know it's the right type of axe from looking at other historical exhibits in the country, but I'm afraid the story written on the card beneath the executioner waxwork uses more than a little creative licence." He looked between us, frowning at Sean's livid expression that came from the new knowledge that the weapon used in the murders could have been identified much earlier, and might have gone undiscovered forever, had I not decided to amuse myself whilst waiting for Sean's phone call to end. "Well, how was I to know? They must have put a heck of a lot of work into restoring it. Say… can I have it back when you find it? Now it will have some real local history attached to it!"

"We should go and look at the exhibit," I said to Sean instead of replying to the owner, sensing that not only was it important for us to see the original home of the axe to gather evidence and better understand the motives of the murderer, it was equally important to remove Sean from the vicinity of a man scatterbrained enough to not bother to call the police when a dangerous weapon went missing from his stash.

The Chamber of Horrors was just the way I remembered it. Fake blood dripped down the walls, somehow still looking sticky. Plastic candles with flickering false flame bulbs illuminated the room, mounted on a chandelier made from an old wagon wheel. Torture devices were everywhere, and there were various gruesome tales pinned to the walls, complete with illustrations of the terrible things that had been done to witches in the past. I observed that none of the stories were actually local, and I wondered if there was a reason why there was no record of any Wormwood witches being caught and punished. Perhaps it was because they'd always been in charge of the town, instead of being a persecuted minority.

"There it is," I said, needlessly pointing to the hooded figure standing proudly beside the guillotine. His hands were stretched upwards, and it was obvious that he should have been holding an axe over his head in a sufficiently menacing manner. I wasn't certain whether axe executions had ever taken place in this part of the country, but it was a familiar idea that people associated with the barbaric side of history. It was a good way to give visitors chills and delight fans of all things horror. After being stolen, the axe had been replaced by a golf club with a tag attached, that read: 'Axe undergoing maintenance'. It definitely didn't have quite the same wow factor.

"More like undergoing a revival," Sean commented, walking closer to the scene.

I glanced down at the information label that Mr Hammond had confessed was mostly pure fabrication.

This axe dates from the 1700s. During its time of service, it was responsible for taking the head of Mary Pickle, a notorious thief, and it is also believed to have been used at the botched execution of Grant Herald - in which the executioner missed his neck and chopped his arm off instead. After capital punishment was banned in the UK, executioners were forced to hang up their hoods and boots. To this day, there are some who want to return to the old customs and believe that the only true justice can be found at the sharp edge of a blade.

"What utter drivel," Sean commented.

"But what do you think? Did someone take these words as inspiration?" I asked him.

My boyfriend remained silent for a long time. His eyes focused on those of the hooded waxwork executioner. I sensed that he was thinking about the victims of the killer and how they must have felt, looking into the eyes of someone standing over them, wielding a weapon that was death itself. "There can't be any more deaths," he said after an age had passed.

I reached out and squeezed his arm, knowing what he was feeling. I shared the same desperation, the same need to stop disaster before it struck again. "I wonder why they feel the need to be the hand of justice in this election?"

"Maybe it's because…" Sean started to say, the crease between his eyebrows deepening as he struggled to grab onto a thread of thought that had fallen from the mass of swirling possibilities in his mind.

"Sorry to bother you," Mr Hammond said, popping his head around the heavy wooden door of the fake dungeon. "I was just wondering if you could be so kind as to sign the guestbook on your way out? I do actually insist upon it, you see. No one escapes having their name on paper - except for those who pop in when I'm busy, but that is a rarity."

"I'm taking the guestbook with me," Sean bluntly informed him.

"Thank you for letting us look around," I said when we walked back past the owner, whose mouth was doing a good impression of a goldfish.

"But… but," he stuttered.

"It will be returned when it's been examined," Sean said, making a grudging effort to be understanding.

"Why would it need to be examined? I sincerely doubt that the axe thief signed their name before robbing me. In fact, I know they didn't because I checked… you know, on the off chance," the older man confessed.

"We're just checking every possible avenue for potential evidence that might help us to solve these recent crimes," I said, hoping that Mr Hammond wouldn't notice Sean's scathing attitude towards him.

"Oh, well… okay. Please take good care of it. I suppose I can crack on with the new book, even though the old one hasn't been filled up yet." Mr Hammond looked pained at the thought of starting something new before the old one had been completed.

Sean wasted no time in flipping open the book after we'd left the shop. He sat down on a bench next to a giant wooden planter that had been installed during one of those 'make Wormwood brighter' campaigns. It was the sort of policy that Rhiannon Garda was running on, and I wondered how much support she was generating and what the town might look like if someone who really cared about a greener, brighter town took over. Wormwood could certainly do a lot worse than having her as its mayor.

"Ah-ha!" Sean said, his finger stabbing a page in the book he'd been poring over. "Here are some familiar faces. Anita Heron visited the museum two weeks ago. She left a comment thanking Mr Hammond for taking the time to show her his collection of throwing blades before the charity open day began." He raised his eyebrows. "This open day seems to have attracted a large number of people," he observed flicking through a couple of pages to check where the names ended. "There are several familiar faces. I suppose all of them wanted to be seen to be charitable and caring, prior to putting themselves forward for election," Sean said with a sigh. "Rhiannon Garda commented that she appreciated the support for the charity she'd suggested. Andy Carat just signed his name, so did Ed Brindle and Jesse Heathen."

I frowned. I hadn't even known that Jesse was in Wormwood two weeks ago.

"Lorna Carat is one of the last people to sign in that day, so I doubt she arrived with her husband," he observed.

"Do you think she could have been following him because she suspected he was up to something?" I mused. The dynamics between that couple were incredibly hard to understand. "Has Lorna Carat tried to contact you?" I added when a sudden thought occurred to me.

Sean checked his phone. "No, why?"

"Because I think she received a threat from the killer today," I said, remembering the brown envelope that she'd opened prior to us going upstairs to speak with her husband and the way that she'd frowned at the letter inside. At the time, it hadn't meant anything to me, but both Rhiannon and Jesse had been sent similar envelopes. "Isn't it strange that she hasn't reported it?"

17

THE MISSING LINK

Lorna Carat had strenuously denied receiving any threats when we'd called her at lunchtime.
According to her, Andy hadn't been sent anything like that either. We'd called Jade Rey and asked if she'd received any unexpected post recently, but she'd reassured us that nothing had arrived for her. Hemlock also hadn't been sent any threats, but that was probably because he was a cat and the killer wasn't taking him seriously. I hadn't told him that because I knew he would have done something to make them take him seriously, and a killer with a vendetta against a cat was the last thing Sean and I needed in this complicated enough ongoing crime spree.

Actually, that wasn't true. The last thing we needed was for the candidates to get together to hold a candlelight vigil for the two deceased men. A vigil that Rhiannon had been threatened into organising, the real purpose of which was undoubtedly to give the killer another chance to strike or make more threats. This time, Sean had demanded a fully uniformed police presence in the hopes that it might put the killer off their game, but we both knew it was mostly for show. Yet again, we found ourselves one step behind the axe murderer.

When evening fell and a small crowd gathered to support the candidates and the hastily put together event, Rhiannon took to the stage. She thanked everyone for coming to the vigil she'd organised in memory of Ed Brindle and Graham Jinx. Then, with poise that I couldn't help but admire, she confessed that she was a hypocrite and had worked for environmentally unfriendly companies in the past. She apologised for not being transparent and promised that she was just as dedicated to her policies as ever.

Jade Rey walked over to us whilst Rhiannon was making her speech. "I still haven't been sent anything by the killer," she said without any preamble. "Does it seem to you like they're winding things down the closer we get to the election? Maybe there aren't any secrets being hidden. Maybe those of us who are left are honest enough for them."

"Maybe the killer is working up to a big finish," I replied through gritted teeth, pretty certain that the mayoral murderer was not going to go out like a damp squib. Things were far more likely to end with a bang.

Sean clearly thought so, too. "The entire square was searched prior to everyone's arrival," he reassured me when Jade had left to stand with the other surviving candidates. "There was no sign of any hidden surprises."

He meant there'd been no bombs or masked murderers hiding in the branches of the trees that ringed Wormwood's square. I shivered a little when I thought of the last time an event involving the Mayor of Wormwood had taken place in this square, but that was all in the past, where history should remain.

The problem is, this killer doesn't agree with that, I thought absentmindedly, as a slideshow of images flashed up on the projector screen that had been erected at the back of the stage. Insipid music featuring pianos and strings played through the PA system. Something important flashed in my mind for a moment, before Jesse Heathen appeared in front of me and the beginning of the idea was banished just as easily as it had arisen.

"I thought you were busy hiding from a giant snake?" I greeted him. Sean walked off in the opposite direction, clearly not in the mood to tolerate the other man tonight.

Jesse scratched the back of his neck and glanced around anxiously. "I've had some time to think, after being stuck in my room, and I've decided that my message as future mayor and giver of hope to the people of Wormwood is too important for me to abandon now. I refuse to hide!" He cleared his throat. "That, and I've decided that they're bluffing. It would take an extraordinary amount of power and effort to summon what they're claiming to be able to summon. Frankly, I think someone has looked into my past, but that's the extent of it. Just because they know who I am and what I'm afraid of doesn't mean they can do anything to make it a reality."

"How courageous of you to show up," I said, not meaning a word of it.

"Well, I owe it to my future constituents," Jesse said unblushingly. "A poll was done recently, and I think I may be in with…"

The sound of many, many animals interrupted him. Just as had happened at the debate, Wormwood's familiars spilled en masse into the town square. Hemlock was once again carried in on a shield. Today, he wasn't wearing his cape or crown, but he was sporting a golden rosette that was somehow staying in place on his chest. He looked fluffier than I'd ever seen him look before. I squinted when the shield was lowered and he ceremoniously withdrew a pre-ignited candle from the in-between, placing it with the others that were already dancing in the night breeze.

"Is he wearing hair extensions? Can cats have hair extensions?" Sean asked, doing some squinting of his own.

I watched as Hemlock was carried away again on his shield. A thunderous applause followed him, along with many comments about how cute he was, and wouldn't it be sweet to have a mayor like him? I patiently waited until he was being swept right past me. Then, I scooped him off his shield using the net I'd just pulled out of the in-between. His convoy continued without realising that their glorious leader had just been catnapped.

"How dare you!" Hemlock complained once he'd realised he was no longer riding a shield. "This is sabotage! You know I'm going to win, so you're sabotaging me! People like you will be outlawed when I'm in office!"

"What have you done to yourself?" I asked my familiar, wisely ignoring everything he'd just said.

Hemlock looked down. "Oh! You mean the fur?"

"No, I mean the ridiculous rosette - yes, the fur!"

Hemlock considered it. "A survey carried out by my minions confirmed than eight out of ten people in Wormwood responded more favourably to my fluffier portraits. When shown a longhaired black cat, they responded even more favourably. It was a pretty simple spell really. Well, simple for those of us who are good at magic," he said smugly with a sideways look at me. I ignored that, too. "It had some words and some powders and stuff. There were some things you didn't have, even though I opened every jar in the shop to check, but I just left them out and it's worked perfectly anyway. I'm the best magical cat ever!"

I inwardly groaned at Hemlock's pronouncement that

he'd opened every jar in the shop. I hadn't failed to noticed that he hadn't said anything about shutting them again.

"This fur is going to win me this election. Those saps will be voting for me in droves! I needed something to give me the edge over that Carat chump, as we were neck and neck in the polling survey that was just taken, and this will definitely do it. Now all I need you to do is ruin his election by framing him for murder, or something like that, and I'll be mayor of this town. I will of course reward your service," he added as an afterthought.

"Wait… there was a survey? And you were nearly in the lead?!" The second sentence was said with a great deal more alarm than the first.

Jesse laughed, having heard my last comment. "Oh yes, there was a survey done by the town hall employees. A pretty good one, too, considering everything that's been going on and the updates that were required along the way." Here, to my disapproval, he mimed chopping an axe.

"And what happened?" I asked, alarmed that this had somehow passed me by. I supposed I'd been too focused on the investigation to consider how the election was actually progressing. It seemed secondary when there was a murderer running rampant.

"I came third. Andy and Hemlock were too close to call. Rhiannon's a close fourth - or she was until she had to confess to her not so green past today - and Lorna and Jade are trailing behind. It's probably because everyone now knows Jade makes weapons for fun, and they think she's the murderer. People think Lorna is too obsessed with ruining her husband's campaign to consider voting for her," he said for the last woman, giving a casual shrug.

"I can't believe that Hemlock might be leading this election," I muttered, horrified in the extreme. That was yet another thing I'd missed by becoming too closely involved with this investigation. With so much support, it was going to be very difficult to stop Hemlock from marching to victory. On the one hand, I remained impressed that he'd committed to doing something and had followed through with it, but on the other hand, I knew that - whilst Wormwood's residents might think they were voting for the silkiest-haired cat in England - all of that extra long fur concealed a power hungry tyrant within. For all of his talk, Hemlock had never actually been handed power prior to now, which is what made this election so concerning.

Wormwood did not know what it was letting itself in for.

"I can't believe that anyone below fourth place would even bother to turn up for the election," Jesse contributed. "At least Lorna must have seen the results of the survey, because she's not here."

I frowned and looked around at the crowd, which had increased in size as other town residents turned up to pay their respects to the deceased and join together as they hoped for an end to these crimes and for justice to be done. I could see Andy Carat, Jade Rey, and Rhiannon Garda standing closer to the candles and the slideshow projected onto the screen, which alternated between images of both of the men who'd died. Jesse was by my side and Hemlock was currently trying to cut his way out of the net using a pair of scissors he'd pulled from the in-between.

Lorna Carat was definitely not here.

I signalled to Sean across the square, pointing to the candidates, and then the two who were by me, making my expression questioning. Sean glanced around and frowned, also noticing Lorna Carat's absence. He moved through the throng of people towards Andy Carat, undoubtedly to ask if he knew why his wife wasn't in attendance at a vigil that was almost obligatory for the candidates to attend to show that they had cared about their competitors.

He didn't make it as far as Andy before the music changed to the theme tune from *Mission Impossible* and a video flashed up on the screen, replacing the images of the men we were here to remember.

"What is that?" I heard someone say as the audience squinted at the dark image on screen. The person responsible for the video must have changed something because the picture suddenly came into focus and a bright room appeared with an even more brightly lit spot at the centre of the floor. Nothing moved in the room, and it seemed as though the video had been paused, or perhaps replaced with a photo - a photo I assumed meant nothing to any of us. I took advantage of the lull to leave Hemlock and Jesse behind and approached the screen to stand with the candidates and Sean.

"That's… that's the storage barn I'm renting," Andy said, his voice just audible to me. I shot him a curious look, before the image moved and Lorna Carat appeared on screen.

She looked left and right, as if afraid that someone was watching her, before walking across the room to the row of filing cabinets. *It's behind you!* I thought, in the manner of a pantomime audience, willing her to look back at the camera that was filming her every move. "Doesn't she know the camera is there?" I asked Andy in as low a voice as I could manage.

"There are no cameras in the storage barn," he said.

A fresh chill ran over my body as I remembered the brown envelope I'd seen Lorna holding, and then her strenuous denial of ever receiving a threat - even though I was now certain she had been sent one. *What exactly was written on that letter?* I wondered.

"What is she doing?" Sean asked, joining us.

We watched as Lorna took out a key that had been hidden behind a painting of a seascape that hung on the wall behind the cabinets.

"That is some bad security," Sean observed.

"The storage barn is safe enough. It's just an added precaution," Andy replied through gritted teeth.

I noticed that both his reply and facial expressions were remarkably tense for a man whose wife is being filmed going through a filing cabinet in their own storage barn. She hadn't broken in anywhere, but Andy looked like he was sweating bullets.

"What is she doing?" he hissed, apparently to himself, as his wife opened the drawer and swiftly thumbed through the files inside. She found the one she was looking for and lifted it out, opening the brown folder to reveal some papers inside. Here, the camera zoomed in, giving everyone in the audience a glimpse of what looked like a formally written letter.

The video vanished and the screen went black for two seconds.

Didn't get a good look?

Here's a close up.

The picture changed again and now a photo of part of a letter appeared. The name of a firm of lawyers had been printed at the top.

Dear Mr Carat,

Please be advised that our legal team has been retained by Frank Jessop and Harry Bright to investigate and take legal action against you for defamatory remarks and deceitful methods used by you against our clients in order to secure their subsequent dismissal from Free Tech International Corporation, where you are currently employed as a consultant.

Mr Jessop and Mr Bright claim that you falsified computer records to remove their work from the company's servers. They further claim that you then produced their work as your own and took credit for it, securing yourself a promotion that had been contested by the three of you.

Mr Jessop and Mr Bright have ample evidence of the record changes that you made, and reports of defamatory remarks you made to other colleagues and superiors in order to encourage their dismissal and your own advancement.

Your words and actions have caused irreparable damage to the reputations of our clients and we will be seeking full compensation for the harm you have inflicted.

It took a while before everyone in the audience had read through the letter, but when they had, all eyes turned towards Andy Carat. Eyes that were wide with shock and accusation.

"I guess that's why your wife complained to me that you were responsible for your family's poor financial situation," Jesse said, having sidled over to where the drama was taking place. "She implied you'd done something stupid and driven by ego, but she wouldn't say exactly what it was."

Andy had turned pale. "That letter is private! It's been resolved since. It was just a misunderstanding! I'm ambitious, but I'm not a psychopath," he said, looking like a ghost of the confident man I'd first seen at the candidate announcement event. He shot hounded looks left and right, knowing how this looked… knowing that people would be drawing parallels between the lengths he'd gone to in order to secure a promotion, and the lengths that the mystery murderer was going to in order to claim the position of mayor.

I knew that I was certainly drawing those parallels.

"Why would she do this?" Andy said. "We've always done everything important together."

"Do you think she's feigning not knowing she's being filmed? Could she have set this up to get back at her husband?" Sean whispered into my ear.

"Jesse did say she was trailing in a local polling survey," I whispered back, but I wasn't convinced. If that was the case, why fail to report the threat she'd received to the police, which would have made her actions now seem more credible? Covering it up made me think that the letter had warned her not to say anything and that her current actions were not something she had elected to do out of her own free will, but something she'd been instructed to do. The question was, by whom?

"Those papers and the court ruling that followed are private! That was part of the deal!" Andy complained, looking nervously around at the audience. "The court ruled that my ambition had got the better of me. I have to pay compensation, which isn't pleasant or cheap, but I'm doing it. I don't understand why Lorna would do this to me. I know we're currently competing, but we always have rules that can't be broken. Some things remain between us."

"She might have imagined she was protecting you," I suddenly suggested, thinking about Lorna's furtive looks left and right when she'd entered the room. It was as if she'd been concerned that someone might be in there with her… concerned that someone might have got there before her.

"You think she was tricked into behaving suspiciously when the killer already had the documents?" Sean said, considering the idea himself. "It does sound plausible." He took my arm and we walked out of earshot of people like Andy and Jesse. "Do you think someone is out to get Andy, and why?"

"He didn't receive a threat of his own," I commented, glancing back at the man. "And I don't know about anyone being out to get him specifically. It's not as if he's the only one this has happened to. It doesn't seem like anyone's emerged from this unscathed."

We watched as Anita Heron walked over to him, her hand trembling with what I was almost certain was a combination of nerves and bravery over being the first one to comfort the man, who'd just had something he'd imagined had been put to bed long ago dredged up and displayed for all to see. *Someone has certainly done their homework!* I thought, remembering Rhiannon's forced confession, Jesse's serpent scare, and now Andy's exposure. The killer was good at finding things out. The question was, how did they do it, and why? Why this rabid pursuit of 'the truth' and a refusal to let anyone conceal anything about their pasts? Whom did it serve, and what might have driven them to become a fanatic?

I was still considering the possible answers to these questions when one of the police officers walked over and showed Sean their iPad. "I recorded the video on this," he said, offering it to his boss. "I thought you might want a second look."

Sean blinked, but he took the iPad with the video playing and dutifully looked at it with his eyes glazed over. I knew that he was thinking about other things, a thousand thoughts and theories, so I found myself watching it for him.

And I noticed something alarming.

"Andy, when did you last see your wife?" I called to him,

dashing over and interrupting Anita Heron's attempts to comfort the distraught candidate, who'd suddenly found himself facing suspicion instead of the adoration he was used to.

Jesse sidled over again and whispered in my ear. "He should have been honest about being a baddie from the start. Just look at me, people respect my past because I don't hide it. Makes you wonder what else he's hiding, doesn't it?"

I pretended to ignore Jesse, but his words did make me think. They made me wonder if even now, Andy had a backup plan that would see him shrug off this apparent exposure of his dark past. It made me wonder if the killer was targeting themselves in the most dramatic fashion possible in a clever double bluff to shrug off any real suspicion directed at them. *He told me that the only competition he was concerned about were the other male candidates* - that was what Lorna Carat had said when she'd taken to the stage to announce her candidacy. Now, two male competitors were dead.

The question was, did Andy have some cards up his sleeve?

The previous favourite for mayor blinked. "I don't know. I think I saw her at lunch time and then she went out. Yes… it was at lunch." He shook off his unfocused speech halfway through. I found myself carefully considering whether it was another rehearsed piece, another preplanned play designed to get the right reaction.

"Are there any windows in your storage building?" I asked, feeling my heartbeat quicken when I reached the more important question.

Andy considered. "Yes, there are some fairly high up in the large open-plan space. Lorna was upstairs in the office storage area in the video. That room is fully enclosed, but there is a skylight."

I felt the blood drain from my face. I rushed back over to Sean. "The video…" I said, hearing a pounding in my ears as the sensation that something terrible had happened overtook me completely "…it wasn't live. It was pre-recorded." I pointed to the bright spot on the floor of the room on the screen of the iPad. "That's the light from the skylight. All of this happened much earlier today."

Sean's expression grew grim. "She might already be dead," he said, voicing my fears out loud.

As one, we looked over towards Anita Heron, who was still pawing at Andy.

"Who do we know who has something to gain from clearing a path for Andy to become mayor, making it appear as if his wife has betrayed him, and finally getting rid of his wife for good?" I said, feeling a heavy weight settle in my stomach. *They always say it's the quiet ones you have to watch out for…* - that was what Anita herself had said to me.

"There might still be time," Sean said, seizing my arm and pulling me after him towards Andy Carat and Anita Heron. "You're coming with me," he announced, swapping my arm for Andy's and frogmarching him towards the car. He pushed the other man onto the backseat and called two uniformed officers over, speaking some inaudible instructions. The police officers made a beeline for Anita Heron.

Right before I got into the car with Sean and Andy, I glanced backwards and got to see Anita Heron's perfectly shocked expression as the officers accosted her.

It's always the quiet ones.

18

RESCUE OR RECOVERY

"Is she dead? That's what you think, isn't it? You think my wife is dead!" Andy said from the backseat of the car, his voice rising to an uncontrolled crescendo at the end.

"Mr Carat, we really need to know the address of the storage barn," Sean said, regarding the man in the seat steadily in the rearview mirror.

"It's Witchwood," he said, sounding numb. "The industrial estate on the outskirts of town. Do you know it? There's a... there's a soft play centre and it's in the same yard as that."

Sean nodded and kept driving, but I could almost read his thoughts. Were we on a rescue or a body recovery mission? And was the man in the backseat an innocent victim, or something else entirely?

I bit my lip and thought of Anita, who'd always seemed to be in such a flap whenever attention was focused on her. I knew that jealousy could make a person do unexpected things. Love, or the perceived idea of love, could be even worse than that. All the same, I discovered I had some serious doubts. One thing kept bothering me about the idea of Anita Heron being the one who was responsible for everything, and it wasn't her mousey personality. The murderer seemed obsessed with dredging up the past. Perhaps Anita Heron didn't believe that anyone had a pure enough past to become the Mayor of Wormwood, which would make sense if she'd done all of this to cling to power herself, but how did Andy fit into that theory? She'd been nothing but supportive of him every time we'd spoken with her. Throwing him under the bus of public opinion by revealing a past littered with legal action and financial ruination didn't seem to fit.

I silently groaned, wondering which piece of the puzzle I was missing. I wondered why the final piece felt like it wasn't even from the same jigsaw.

Andy ripped the back door open and leapt out as soon as we came to a stop outside the breeze block and corrugated metal building that he'd indicated. A light came on above the doors, triggered by the movement of the car. "Lorna!" he yelled at the top of his voice.

Sean slapped the steering wheel in frustration. So much for subtlety.

"Our arrival will have been expected," I said, trying to reassure him that the element of surprise was already non-existent. The killer had been several steps ahead of us since the very start. I frowned as I suddenly remembered Anita being unable to change her script when she'd given the closing speech after the killer's first slideshow at the candidate announcement event. It could have been a ruse to throw us off the scent, but she hadn't shown any signs of being able to adapt, and the killer appeared to be a master of predicting reactions and next moves. Surely someone like that had a certain flair for communication? It had certainly seemed so in the way that the slides, and even the threats, had been worded. When it came to having flair in anything, Anita would be my last pick.

There was, however, one person who had flair by the bucketload, and he was marching up to the barn-style door of the storage building even as Sean and I hesitated, checking out the place before charging in.

I blinked as Sean removed the magic-seeing glasses he'd put on to inspect the building. "This is not what I would call a regular storage unit," he said, commenting on the size. It was large enough to run a car garage. "Makes you wonder what they're storing in there. How much stuff can one couple have? Mr Carat! Wait!" Sean called after the mayoral candidate.

He answered with a desperate look, his hand on the latch of one of the doors. "We have to find her! I have to know! I can't see any spells. No one has boobytrapped anything. Let's just get inside!"

"It's safest to check first, even if there's no magic visible," I said as placatingly as I could. I reached into the in-between, wondering what the mysterious space knew about the situation I found myself in and what it would supply to help me.

"Why are you holding a stick with a pointing rubber hand on the end?" Andy asked.

I didn't respond to him, but instead used the pointing finger to lift the latch on the door, before hooking it under the latch and pulling. The barn door swung outwards easily, the hinges barely complaining.

Nothing moved or jumped to attack.

No historically inaccurate guillotine blades dropped.

"Please let us go first. We don't know what might be inside," Sean said. "It's better to be careful and quiet than…"

"Lorna!" Andy yelled into the dark interior where no

light entered, now that night had taken hold. In spite of Sean's request that Andy stay quiet, we all listened to the silence that followed his shout, straining to hear something - anything - that might indicate someone was still alive in here.

"Did you hear that?" Andy said, a tremor in his voice.

We listened again.

There was... something.

"Lorna?" Andy called again, but this time his voice was barely louder than a whisper.

There was a small tapping sound, as if something non-metallic was being brought into contact with metal. The first time, none of us was certain that it was anything other than the metal of the building cooling off after a warm day, but then it came again, more rhythmic and determined.

The lights snapped on after several blinks as the fluorescent tubes got going. I glanced over and discovered that Sean had walked over to the edge of the building in the darkness and found the switch. My eyes turned away to scour the large space I discovered we were in and I realised that, not only was this place big enough for a mechanic to set up shop, it was also being used as a garage. An old VW van was parked to the left, and to the right was an MG Midget that had been completely deconstructed - its parts scattered across a blanket that had been lain on the concrete floor of the storage space. Various other parts of vehicles rested everywhere, like a semi-organised junk yard, and there were two hydraulic car lifts. The one closest to the entrance of the barn was currently holding a red Toyota pickup truck that had certainly seen better days. It was this truck which initially blocked my view of the car on the second lift, raised high above the concrete.

"A Chevrolet Bel Air," Sean said, appearing back at my

side and surprising me with his apparent knowledge of classic cars.

That was when I remembered Andy mentioning this car during his first ever speech. He'd used it as a metaphor for the drastic change Wormwood needed to bring the town into a new era.

"It's cream," I said, before a lot of things slid into place in my brain. "Oh my gosh. He painted it cream."

"Lorna!" Andy screeched when he finally saw his wife. She was lying beneath the raised Chevrolet, bound by ropes and with a gag across her mouth. The sound of something hitting metal had been her feet knocking against one of the legs of the raised platform. He started to run over.

The sound of the door slamming as loudly as a gunshot made all of us jump with shock and spin around.

A woman was standing in the now shut doorway to the barn. There was a large axe in her right hand. In her left hand she held something smaller - *a remote,* I thought.

"Well, here we are at last," Rhiannon Garda said with a horrible smile.

19

CONFESSION OF A KILLER

Andy turned away from her to keep running to his wife.

"Don't!" I yelled, instinct making me whack him across the chest with the rubber hand on a stick to force him to come to a standstill. The stick broke and vanished into the in-between.

"A very wise choice," Rhiannon said, lifting her left hand a little higher. "I've made a few alterations to your car lift. It was easy enough. All I needed to do was loosen a few screws. In fact, I'm not entirely sure how long it will hold up, even without me pushing this button. If you want to help your wife by running over there to free her, you are welcome to try. We can find out if you're faster than a falling car. Or perhaps you'll both be crushed." She looked amused by the prospect. "You know, the great thing about these really old cars is that they were built to last. Isn't that right, Andy? You could probably drive into a wall in one of those beasts, and it would be the wall that wouldn't survive the incident. You could probably drive into a person and only have a few dings to bang out of the metalwork, but that's easy to do on these old vehicles. No one would ever guess you'd killed someone."

"What is she talking about?" Sean asked, standing stiffly beside me with his eyes fixed on the woman with the axe and remote control that both had the potential to end lives.

"He repainted the car," I said in answer to his question, loudly enough for Rhiannon herself to hear. "It used to be crimson, but he repainted it cream to fix the rust problem. Only, it wasn't to fix a rust problem."

Rhiannon raised the axe with a single hand, demonstrating strength that must be derived from her jujitsu and kendo disciplines. "Correct! It was to fix an evidence problem."

"I read a newspaper article about the death of your brother. He was killed by a hit and run driver. There were no witnesses, and the only thing left behind were some flakes of red paint."

Rhiannon raised her eyebrows, wanting me to go on... predicting that I would do the explaining for her.

"I assume that you believe Andy secretly repainted his car after finding out that flakes of paint had been left behind at the scene, in order to stop suspicion from ever falling on him?

Here, Rhiannon snorted. "At the time, he needn't have bothered. The police did almost nothing to look into it. With so little evidence, and no one having witnessed it, they said there was nothing to go on. It wouldn't happen in this day and age, with surveillance cameras everywhere and the advances in modern science, but it did happen back then. Back then, they weren't able to do something like test the paint flakes to find out what type of car it might have come from. Years later, when I read about that kind of thing being done on the internet, I went back to the police and asked them to reopen the case and use the evidence they'd collected. At first, they claimed it had been lost. Then, when I didn't go away, they found the file and the evidence that had been collected and gave it to me, saying that the case was never going to be reopened all of these years later with nothing to go on. They warned me that, even if I did get a significant result from the paint, it would be nothing more than circumstantial evidence, and without anything beyond that and my personal suspicions, a credible case could never be built. They told me to forget about it." She took a deep breath. "I had the paint tested and the results came back a month ago. I've always had my suspicions about who was responsible for my brother's death, but when there's still that fraction of doubt, taking action could be a mistake. Worse still, I could have been wrong and punished an innocent man for the actions of an unknown stranger." Her mouth curved up into a grim smile. "The paint analysis changed all of that. It was confirmed as belonging to a 1952 Chevrolet Styleline Deluxe Bel Air. It's a pretty rare car in these parts, isn't it?" Rhiannon said, looking towards Andy.

"It was imported," he muttered, his affection for classic cars making him respond, even when he knew he was being pushed into a corner.

"All I'd needed was confirmation, and that was it. I hoped that, what with it being such a rare car, it might be enough to convince the police to take another look. It just so happened that the police officer I spoke to on the phone was a classic car fan and regularly went to local meet ups. I told him about the paint results and asked if he knew anyone in the area who owned a car like that. He said that he knew one guy who owned a Bel Air, but it was cream not red. He told me it belonged to a man named Andy Carat, and suggested that he might be able to help me find out if there was another owner in the area who owned a red version of the car. He thought there might even be a chance that the paint could be forensically matched to one car in particular, as paint mixes weren't always consistent back when it was manufactured." She sighed. "Even though the colour of the car was wrong, I knew that I wasn't mistaken about the person responsible. There had to be a logical explanation for the colour change. And then at the first event in the mayoral election…" she laughed bitterly "…he literally confessed to having repainted his car, giving some baloney reason about rust and change making us all stronger. I could not believe his arrogance! At least it left no more doubt in my mind - Andy Carat had got away with murder."

"Murder?" Sean interjected. "You believe it was intentional, rather than say, a young driver having an accident and being afraid that it would ruin his life? It was wrong of the person responsible for your brother's death to stay silent about it, but calling it murder is…"

"…absolutely what it is," Rhiannon said, her voice passionless as she looked at the visibly sweating Andy Carat. "You see, I suspected Andy even before I found out what car he owned all of these years later. Back when it happened, I was in no state to investigate anything. It was only when the years slipped by and I began to look into what had been going on in my brother's life at the time, searching for a motive behind his death that everyone had always denied existed - claiming it was nothing more than a random accident - that I found something important." She stared at Andy, her eyes filled with hate. "This isn't your first election, is it?"

"He was student council president in sixth form," I said, remembering Andy telling us that himself when he'd been boasting to boost the press release I'd pretended to write about him. "It came with a scholarship to university."

Rhiannon nodded, her gaze still fixed on Andy, as if he might disappear and cheat her from getting justice once again. "Guess who was the favourite to win that election?"

"This is all nonsense," Andy said, but his ears were turning pink and his words were halfhearted. I couldn't help thinking about the court case he'd lost. He'd confessed that his ambition had pushed him to go too far in pursuit of something he'd wanted.

It seemed likely that it wasn't the first time it had happened.

"It was my brother, Jim Garda. He was going to run away with that election and land a scholarship, which would have changed his life and set him up for all of the success that he deserved to have." Tears were running down Rhiannon's cheeks now. She didn't relinquish her hold on either the axe or the remote to wipe them away but stood defiant, never looking away from the man she believed was responsible for her misery. "You couldn't let him win, could you? So, you killed him," she said, her voice little more than a whisper all of a sudden.

"This is ridiculous," Andy said, shifting his feet uncomfortably. Beyond that denial, he didn't have anything else to say to support his innocence.

"I understand what you must be feeling with regards to Andy and your brother's fate, but why did you murder two other candidates?" I asked, trying to understand how that made sense in Rhiannon Garda's mind when it certainly seemed hypocritical to me. She claimed she was looking for justice for her brother's murder, but now she'd committed the same sin, twice over.

"It was all for him… for Jim," she said with absolute sincerity.

Sean and I weren't used to confessions slipping easily from the lips of the killers we'd caught, but Rhiannon was being open about everything, apparently not wanting to hide anything. She was even holding the murder weapon. In the back of my mind, a little voice whispered that this wasn't going to have a happy ending.

"It began by chance, really. I'd received the results of the paint sample test and had heard rumours that Andy Carat would be running for mayor, so I decided I would put myself forward, too. I thought a good way to kick it off and get a look at my adversary would be to organise a charity event, which I did with the help of Terence Hammond, who owns that curiosity shop in town. He threw an open day with a silent charity auction, where you write your bids down on a piece of paper. The profits went to the cleaner seas charity I'd chosen. As it was my idea, I turned up early in the day to make sure everything was running smoothly and see if there was anything I could do to help, as well as getting a few photos taken for the local paper. While I was there, two men came in talking loudly about the upcoming election. Out of curiosity, I followed them into the Chamber of Horrors, which is where I heard Ed Brindle talking to Jesse Heathen. Jesse was boasting about being a Norse god and having oodles of power at his fingertips. That was when Ed asked about the possibility of making a devil deal in order to win the election and become mayor."

"I'm sure that did not sit well with you," I said, wanting to encourage her to keep talking whilst I tried to figure out a way out of this situation. I knew that the talking would eventually end and the next move would be played.

With Rhiannon's track record, I didn't fancy my chances of out playing her.

"It certainly did not," she agreed wholeheartedly. "I waited until the scheming pair had left, but not before they'd shared the details of the meeting they were planning to have at the Devil's Jumps in Wormwood Forest. When I emerged from my hiding place, I wasn't sure what action I would take against Ed Brindle. I suppose I was thinking about telling the local council and hoping that they would boot him out of the election, but there would only be my word against his and it could mar my own campaign and cause. Then, I saw the label in front of the executioner display. 'The only true justice can be found at the sharp edge of a blade'," she quoted. "It was... inspiring. I came back when I knew Terence would be on his lunch break and left with the axe. I'd have preferred it if there'd been a sword. That's the weapon I've trained with, but it wasn't too hard to pick up the technique.

"I arrived early at the Jumps that night, not entirely certain of what I was going to do. All I knew was that I was angry. I was angry with Andy Carat and anyone else who thought that they could cheat in an election and get away with it. That was why I scattered the silver coins to signify the betrayal of the principles a good mayor should have. That, and I predicted it would make him bend down to take a closer look, and my axe research and practice had demonstrated that the axe I'd restored to sharp-edged perfection was far easier to use on a downward swing," she added more pragmatically, before a strange little smile played on her lips. "It worked rather well."

"What about Graham? All he did was share a less than brilliant past regret," I said, still hoping that Rhiannon might begin to question her own actions, which were far from beyond reproach.

"You saw what he did! I left it there for you to see. He was a criminal and he was getting away with it." Rhiannon blinked when she said it, and for a moment, I thought she might have had a flash of insight that it was during this murder when her fanaticism had spiralled beyond her control. "That, and I knew Andy was in the library, too. I hoped he would hear what happened to Graham and tremble, knowing that his own past regret was not the truly terrible regret I was certain he must be carrying around with him. I thought that it might scare him into telling the truth." Here, she paused and shot a scathing look in Andy's direction. "Now, I'm not convinced he regrets it at all. My brother was just another stepping stone for him on his way to success."

"Don't you feel any remorse over Graham's death?" I asked, still gently probing for that rational thought I hoped might return in a sudden flood of realisation.

"Oh, yes. I feel terrible about what happened. If any of my kendo teachers could have seen me, I'd be back with the beginners in half a second. I thought I could handle the axe on a horizontal swing, but it twisted and didn't make it all the way through." She shook her head, regretting the failings of her own ability, rather than the taking of a life. "The next swing was even worse. It went off at an angle, hit the bookshelf, and got stuck. I had to have a third strike and hit the bookshelf again. Still, I got there in the end."

"Couldn't you have spoken to Andy and asked him if he was responsible? Surely you could have appealed to his conscience?" I said, trying to keep her attention and ignore Sean, who was subtly trying to edge away from me towards something I couldn't see.

Rhiannon looked at me like I was crazy. "You really think he would have come clean about it? Even now, when I have the evidence against him in my pocket, he won't tell the truth. At least I told the truth about my past. I came clean about working for those companies who were doing such terrible things to the environment."

"You pretended to have been forced into it by a threat

you sent to yourself," I said, not exactly impressed by her feigned attack of conscience.

"But I used recycled paper and envelopes to send the threats. I even recycled the coffee cup Graham had abandoned on the table in the library." She shook her head. "I was a bit shaken after that one... putting it in the recycling calmed me down."

"You work as a computer programmer, don't you?"

"I genuinely did do some work for the same company Andy works for. That's what you're wondering, isn't it? If that part was true?" Rhiannon said, proving how good she was at thinking a step ahead of everyone else. "I used that opportunity to access the company's servers and discovered the formal complaints that had been lodged against Andy, which handed me the details of the lawyers the past employees with grievances had used. Then, it was so very simple to hack into the law firm's system - they were using an unsecured wifi network, for goodness' sake - and find the letters they'd sent to Andy and the final judgement against him." She tilted her head to one side. "People don't realise how much of their personal information is available online, if you know how to access it. Everyone still has this idea that files stay on their computer, inaccessible to anyone but a person physically in front of their computer. They forget that these days most things are automatically uploaded to the cloud. That has made everything so much easier for people like me." She sighed happily. "Seeing as I doubted Andy was going to confess willingly, and the dolt still hadn't figured out that all of this was supposed to be terrifying him and making him look inside himself and see his own flaws reflected back at him in the men who'd died, I realised I needed to make one last play. I sent out the threats. One for me, to throw anyone suspicious off the scent, one to the boasting man who thinks he's a deity to see if he believed his own waffle, and one to Lorna Carat, to find out how much she cared about her husband's reputation."

"What did the threat say?" I asked, knowing we were getting close to crunch time. I hoped Sean had some bright ideas because I certainly didn't.

"Oh, it wasn't one of my best. I just said something along the lines of, if Lorna didn't collect the court documents from the storage unit I knew she and her husband had rented (this place was simple to find once I'd accessed Lorna's emails) then the axe murderer of Wormwood would be breaking-in at the same time a candlelight vigil was going to be held in Wormwood, taking the documents, and publishing them." Another smile danced on her lips. "I then organised the vigil, knowing it would make the threat more credible in Lorna's eyes. I set up the camera to film her in the office and I waited to catch her when she tried to leave, knowing she would arrive earlier in the day." Rhiannon shot me a cool look. "Because of course, I'd already broken into this place, found that they'd kept paper records of the documents the lawyers had uploaded to their cloud computing service, and had planned exactly what I was going to do to Lorna and how this was going to end. I figured you might care enough about your wife for this to work. It's been so many years... so many years of not knowing for sure. Not knowing who killed my brother." Now, her gaze found Andy. "I am going to give you an opportunity you never gave Jim. You can tell the truth, right here and right now, and I will let your wife live."

I gulped, immediately noticing that she hadn't said anything about Andy's continued survival - but then, why bring an axe if she intended to let everyone walk out of here in the same number of pieces they'd walked in?

Andy opened his mouth. "You're crazy…" he began but another voice cut him off.

"For crying out loud, Andy! Shut up and tell her the truth! She already knows everything," Lorna said, having finally worked her gag loose. "I have lied for you and followed your lead more times than I can count and now, when my life is on the line, you aren't willing to back down? The ego on you is unreal! This is it, Andy. I have finally had it. I know I said the same thing back when you flung us into financial ruin to get a promotion that didn't even land you a better pay packet - just a stupid title and more work - but this time, I mean it." She made a sound of frustration as she wriggled in her bonds and discovered they were just as tight as ever. "I'll tell you everything. I was in the car at the time. I told him to stop when he saw your brother crossing the road, but he wouldn't. He just sped up. By the time I tried to take the wheel from him, it was too late, and anyway, I was too weak to have made a difference. That's why I took up powerlifting. I never wanted to feel weak in a situation like that again." She strained against her ropes, but there were some trials that couldn't be overcome with brute strength, and in any case, Rhiannon would have known about the powerlifting - because she seemed to know everything. I was willing to bet she'd taken a great deal of care with the way she'd tied up Lorna Carat.

"I'm sorry. I really am," Lorna said to Rhiannon. "I'm really only guilty of loving the wrong man. Back then, after it happened, he told me we would be together forever, if I just stood by him, and I did. I have done. Over and over again." She clenched her teeth with the effort of craning her head to make eye contact with the woman holding death in her hands. "I'll testify against him. I'll be a witness. I will do whatever it takes to help you to get justice for your brother to make up for staying silent for all of these years."

I held my breath, knowing it was a confession, but not from the person Rhiannon had wanted to hear it from. By contrast, Andy was uncharacteristically silent, apparently struck dumb by his wife giving in. His expression was stony and devoid of any visible remorse. I thought I could see why Rhiannon had been driven to the edge of her sanity by this man, as well as by the crime he'd committed against her brother.

I looked back at Rhiannon, watching her face as she considered the proposal. A second later, the thoughtful look vanished and she smiled. My heart skipped a beat. "No," she said, sending my stomach tumbling downwards. "You'll recant as soon as you're out from beneath there. Even if you did cooperate out of a very delayed sense of duty, it still might not be enough. He won't admit what he's done, and your testimony, the car paint, and a motive involving a school election and a scholarship programme would probably leave a jury with reasonable doubt. After all - even I wasn't completely certain until he told everyone about the car's colour change. The police were right. The case is dead in the water. Now all that's left is to make him feel a fraction of the pain I've experienced," she said and pressed the button.

And I ran without a clue about what I was going to do to avert certain disaster.

If it hadn't been for the parts of the car lift that Rhiannon had claimed she'd loosened in order to make it fall instead of lower down sticking, just a little bit, I would have been too late. I used that tiny hesitation to reach into the in-between and suddenly discovered I was holding a large metal pole with two square plates on either end. I just had time to curse the in-between for not offering a safe and simple alternative, before I was sliding underneath a ton of metal that was on its way to crash into the floor in a devastating impact.

I shut my eyes when the metal underbelly of the car collided with the makeshift support the in-between had handed me. I was afraid that the support would merely punch a hole through the chassis and the car would continue to fall, crushing both of us, but the spread of the top and the base were wide enough, and the metal held.

But not for long.

I seized the ropes around Lorna, using them to propel her outside of the confines of the car lift, before diving after her. An instant later, the metal support crumpled under the weight and the car tipped to one side, and then the other, before crashing to the ground on tyres that Rhiannon had flattened to make triple sure that the falling car actually crushed her intended victim.

Rhiannon was good at troubleshooting her murder plans… which was why when I turned back to see what was going on behind me, I felt completely helpless.

Sean had intervened with what must have been Rhiannon's attempt to wipe Andy off the political map and the planet. He'd managed to get his hands on a crowbar that had been left propped up against one of the ancient engine blocks littered around the garage area, and he was parrying blows from the axe. The axe was unwieldy, due to its size, but Rhiannon wasn't trying to chop pieces off Sean, and was instead using it like a staff… a staff with a fatally sharp edge.

I bit my tongue to keep from crying out and inadvertently distracting Sean at a crucial moment. I knew that my boyfriend could handle himself in a fight, but I'd seen Rhiannon's martial arts in action. She was formidable.

I tore my gaze away for just a second to see what Andy

was doing, hoping against hope that he was rushing to join the fray and that two against one might tip the balance in Sean's favour.

He was standing in the same place he'd been prior to the action kicking off, staring into the distance with a vague frown on his face. *Has he lost his mind?!* I wondered, before Sean's fight became a tussle and then - all of a sudden - a tumble behind the VW van. The sparring pair disappeared from view.

I heard the sound of metal on concrete.

Then metal being scraped along the car.

Finally... there was silence.

"Sean?" I called out, knowing instinctively that the time for distraction was over. The fight was finished, but who had won?

Sean's head appeared around the side of the camper van. Thankfully, it was still attached to his body.

"How did you win?" I asked, marvelling at the dishevelled looking Rhiannon, whose hands were cuffed behind her back.

"He tripped me up," she complained.

Sean raised an eyebrow. "I cheated. Sometimes, it's the only way you can win a fight you don't deserve to win on paper," he explained with no little sense of irony, given what had happened in the current election and in an election that had taken place many, many years ago.

Sean called for backup. It wasn't long before Rhiannon was in custody and Andy had been led away to be questioned. I wondered if he would repent after all and come clean about the hit and run that I genuinely believed - after Rhiannon had presented the evidence that had been left at the scene and the evidence of his character - had been committed by him in order to win an election and gain a scholarship.

I doubted it.

Even when his wife's life had been in grave danger, he'd stayed silent. Perhaps it could have been shock that had made him unable to speak, but I wasn't convinced. And I hoped I wasn't the only one who'd finally seen Andy's true colours.

"Thank you for saving me," Lorna said, walking away from the police officers who'd undone her bonds and set her free. "You didn't have to do it - put yourself in danger like that. You could have been killed, too, but... I'm glad you saved me," she finished with a shaken smile.

I nodded and let the silence between us hang for a moment, knowing that there was something else she wanted to say.

"Even though she tried to kill me, I meant what I said about owning up about what happened to Jim Garda, and I meant what I said about Andy. We're over and done with. Maybe Rhiannon's right, and justice can't ever officially be done, but... I doubt he'll ever be dabbling in politics or being promoted ever again when I'm finished with him," she promised. "People will know the truth, even if it costs me just as much as it will cost him. I know you're probably wondering about my sudden change of heart, but when she offered him that choice and he just stood there..." She inhaled angrily. "Everything I have ever felt for him evaporated. So, I suppose I just wanted to say, I'll do what I can to help. Just let me know," she said, before allowing herself to be led away to get in a police car and give a statement.

I looked down at the axe that had been abandoned on the garage floor where it had fallen from Rhiannon Garda's hands, waiting for the forensic team to come and collect it. *Some people are haunted by the past,* I reflected. *And then there are others who really ought to be.*

20

MAYORS AND MYSTICAL MAGICAL ITEMS

Wormwood had been left reeling after the two murders and the rumours that one of the favourites to win the election may have been the driver in an unsolved hit and run incident, which had resulted in the death of a young man. Lorna Carat had been true to her word and had spoken up about her part in witnessing and concealing the hit and run, but with Rhiannon herself having confessed to murder, the absence of Andy's confession, and the ease with which a defence lawyer would be able to claim that Lorna had clearly been coerced upon fear of death into telling her story, it looked like justice was never going to be done for Jim Garda - and that had not sat at all well with me. I knew it was one of those things in life that isn't quite right, but instead of a prison sentence and a plea for forgiveness, those of us who believed Andy Carat was guilty of causing deliberate death by dangerous driving judged him by the content of his character, and the judgement was not favourable. I hadn't been at all surprised to hear that the old vicarage where the Carats had lived had been put up for sale just one week after the drama in the garage and the murderer being apprehended. It pained me to think of Lorna and Andy starting their lives again somewhere new, where no one was aware of what they'd done - even if they were separate lives, as Lorna had promised. All I could hope was that Andy's deeds would one day catch up with him, but I knew most people would say that it was just another sign that there was no justice in the world.

I thought that there was justice, but it didn't always arrive in the way we expect it, or sometimes even want it.

Anita Heron had spoken with the local council about potentially postponing the election, but while they'd agreed that the town couldn't go to the polls just days after such a huge scandal and the withdrawal of three candidates, they'd only agreed to extend the election for a week. With a mere three candidates left in the running, it hadn't felt like the people of Wormwood had much of a selection to choose from.

When it came to picking the best of a not so brilliant bunch, Jade Rey had been the only viable option in my books. Unfortunately, her open love for weaponry had hardly made her popular after everything that had befallen the other candidates. No one had fancied a mayor who liked to wave around sharp objects.

In spite of Jesse's best efforts, even prior to the big reveal, he'd been in third place in the survey that Hemlock had been so excited about. It was true that without Andy Carat in the race, Jesse might have benefitted from some extra votes, but something had told me that all of the violence, and the lies and flaws of the human candidates, would make the vote fall in my furry familiar's favour.

I was proud of Hemlock.

He'd decided to pursue something, and he had done it sincerely and with a level of commitment I hadn't ever seen from him before. I'd told him to get a hobby a while ago, and whilst he'd toyed with various whims, including taxidermy, nothing had stuck. Most of his hobbies had merely been Hemlock seeing how far he could try my patience. I strongly suspected that this whole running for mayor idea had started in the same way, but somewhere along the line, he'd started to take it seriously. Posters had been plastered all over the town in the run up to the election, and visits to the apothecary had spiked with people wanting to see the cat running for mayor. Originally, they'd wanted to *touch* the cat running for mayor, but several clawing incidents later, I'd been forced to erect a sign warning visitors not to pet the cat - because he considered himself to be superior to humans and did not appreciate them besmirching his godly aura.

Weirdly, that had made him even more popular.

It had almost been a shame to sabotage him.

Almost.

At first, I'd been relieved when Anita Heron had managed to convince the local council that, as well as pushing back the day of the vote, they should reopen the applications for mayoral candidates to join the race. I'd hoped that it would be the solution to the growing 'Hemlock as Mayor of Wormwood' issue.

I really shouldn't have been so shocked that no one new had thrown their name into the ring.

The killer may have been caught, but taking on the job of mayor had become something cursed. No one had wanted to touch it with a bargepole.

When there'd only been days remaining before the polls opened, Jesse had made a return to his charismatic self and had somehow regained a lot of favour in town. Hemlock had gone for yet more blowdries. It had been obvious that Jade Rey stood no chance of winning.

To make matters worse, both Jesse and Hemlock had realised who their greatest competition was and had begun a petty campaign of sabotage against each other. Jesse had slapped stickers all over Hemlock's posters that had claimed Hemlock's first decree would be to force everyone in Wormwood to worship cats, or be made into cat food as punishment for disobedience. Hemlock had thought that actually might not be a bad idea, until I'd reminded him he was supposed to be the *nice* cat - whose main goal was to look sweet and not be a political tyrant.

"That comes after the election when all promises are broken," Hemlock had said when I'd explained this to him, proving he certainly had learned a thing or two about politics.

Hemlock had retaliated against Jesse by burning his house down.

Or at least, that's the way Jesse had tried to describe it. I happened to know that what had really happened was that Hemlock had set off a banger outside of Jesse's door just when he'd opened it. Jesse was still jumpy after the snake threat and had looked comically terrified…

…which was something that Hemlock had photographed and shared online - captioning it scathingly.

I'd bitten my nails over the outcome, wondering which would have been worse - a devious devil, or a power-crazed cat running things in Wormwood? I'd tried to remind myself that mayors generally didn't have a huge amount of influence over day to day life, but the previous mayor had certainly managed to change that, and only a fool would underestimate either of the two leading candidates.

After tossing and turning for many nights over that prospect, I'd finally had a flash of inspiration. It had been out of sheer desperation, and with a silent prayer for the future of the town, that I had visited one of Wormwood's most popular businesses and appealed to its owner.

Tristan Coltrain had not been keen on the idea.

Knowing what the alternative would be, I hadn't taken his first no as a final answer. I hadn't taken the second or third no either and had instead embarked on a campaign of my own to convince him to at least put his name forward, even if he didn't actually do any campaigning. When he'd argued that there was no way he would have time for that, I'd countered by telling him that Aunt Linda had developed a real flair for baking and missed helping him out. I'd also promised that I would help him with his mayoral duties, should it still prove to be too much. I would be there with him all the way.

He'd accused me of abusing my position as the supposedly impartial local press representative by forcing him to run. I'd told him that my impartial view was that Wormwood desperately needed someone sensible at the helm.

In the end, I'd won. Two days before the town had gone to the polls, Tristan Coltrain had entered the race to become mayor. There'd been no time for posters or a campaign plan, but his name was well known to all in Wormwood, thanks to his very successful Bread Cauldron Bakery. Those with magical abilities knew that he wasn't one of them, and he'd never advertised his knowledge of the existence of magic - even after coming to terms with it - but that didn't seem to make a difference to the people I'd spoken to in the run up to the vote. After a mayor who'd coveted magic and abused it, Wormwood's residents had seemed keen to have a mayor who wasn't going to run rampant with power. Just like me, they'd wanted weird Wormwood to have someone *normal* in control.

The relief had been palpable when Tristan's name had been added to the ballot papers. Even though I'd got jitters when Hemlock had set up a stall in the town square and had briefly opened a 'Familiars Rule!' petting zoo (where everyone in town could come and pet a future local council or mayoral candidate) when the results had been announced, Tristan was the person that most of Wormwood had voted for.

Jade Rey had been gracious in defeat, applauding Tristan and congratulating him on his new position. Jesse and Hemlock had been far from gracious, stalking away through the crowd to lick their wounds.

When I'd gone looking for Hemlock later, I'd found him sitting on a kerb with Jesse - Jesse with a bottle of whisky and Hemlock with a cup of milk that the in-between had undoubtedly supplied him out of pity. Even though Hemlock couldn't be understood by Jesse, both of them had been complaining loudly and lamenting the election that was stolen from them.

I'd allowed myself a gratuitous eye roll at their drama queen antics before approaching. "I heard that there's a new ice-cream place that's just opened up on the other side of town. Do either of you fancy some ice-cream? My treat," I'd added, thinking that - all things considered - both sore losers had put a lot of time and effort into the mayoral race, and someone should acknowledge their hard work.

The previously prickly pair had looked at each other before nodding, finally united on an issue.

"By the way, I'm sticking around," Jesse said when we were sitting at a table out on the street with our ice-cream selections. The flavour special of the week had been tuna (it was one of those places that thought ice-cream could be improved by making it taste like anything but ice-cream) which Hemlock had been delighted with. Judging by the large serving he'd been given, I thought he might well be the only fan of the flavour.

"In Wormwood?" I asked, my eyebrows shooting up as I looked at him over my triple chocolate fudge sundae.

Jesse toyed with his banana split, which had been arranged like a smiley face. "That's what sticking around usually means - staying in one place. I know I didn't get the job as mayor, but that doesn't mean there's nothing here for me. There are many other plans I could put into place. There's so much I could offer."

"Like what?" I asked, doing my best to keep the suspicion out of my voice. In the past, Jesse had feigned setting up a private detective agency and had made deals with the locals that had nearly resulted in the town ceasing to exist all together. Now that things were getting back to normal - by Wormwood's standards at least - the idea of Jesse remaining in town to mess it all up again did not exactly fill me with hope and joy.

"Lots of things," he said with a smile that I didn't like at all. "How's life with ol' Sean? Did you two sort everything out?" he asked with mock concern.

"Not that it's any of your business, but yes. Everything is fine."

Jesse chewed his banana thoughtfully before swallowing. "I knew it would be. I only wanted to push things along a bit. You shouldn't let a mystical magical item and a nasty curse come between you."

I paused with my spoon halfway towards my mouth. A blob of cream fell off and landed on Hemlock's head. "You didn't say anything about the curse when you told me Sean had inherited a property from the victim of a crime, and heavily implied that he'd somehow abused his position to get something he wasn't entitled to! And what mystical magical item are you talking about?!"

Jesse rubbed his chin and pretended to go all thoughtful. "Didn't I mention the curse? Gosh. I certainly *meant* to mention that there happens to be some sort of curse attached to the old place. I believe that there's actually a local legend about the mystical item the curse was put there to protect. Or should I say… put there to contain. It's amazing the things you hear."

"It's amazing the things you keep to yourself when it suits your purpose," I growled. "You haven't changed at all!"

Jesse sat back and grinned. "Why change when I'm already perfect?"

"Hear hear," Hemlock agreed, combing the cream from his ridiculously long fur and shooting me furious looks. There would undoubtedly be an act of revenge to watch out for later.

I put both elbows on the table and leaned closer to the devil who seemed to be on a mission to make my life more difficult. "Jesse, I want to know everything you know about the curse and the mystery item in Sean's house. Everything - not just the parts that you feel like telling me in order to manipulate a desired response."

"What if telling you everything is exactly what I want to do in order to get a desired response?"

It was a marvel that none of Wormwood's psychopaths had got around to murdering Jesse yet.

I pretended to frown with the effort of remembering something. "Isn't there a snake that can be summoned? A snake that you're deathly afraid of?"

Jesse's frown was very genuine. "That is not playing fair. You don't know what you're saying."

"Then put me right on one thing at least. Tell me everything that you know about Sean's house."

Jesse nodded, flipping his palms upwards in a gesture of surrender. "I actually don't know much more than what I've just mentioned. The only other thing I'm aware of is that the curse will eventually kill the person who owns the house. There has never been an exception to that fate throughout the property's history. Whatever the person who gave it to Sean might have told him, it wasn't a gift he should have accepted. Perhaps the previous owner did it with good intentions, believing that there was something different about Sean that will stop the curse from manifesting this time. Or, perhaps Sean wasn't the knight in shining armour he might have believed himself to be at the time and the previous owner wished him ill. Either way, it doesn't really matter." Here, Jesse paused, his mouth curving upwards as his amber eyes rested on mine. "Sean is doomed, and there is nothing you can do about it."

BOOKS IN THE SERIES

Mandrake and a Murder
Vervain and a Victim
Feverfew and False Friends
Belladonna and a Body
Aconite and Accusations
Dittany and a Death
Heliotrope and a Haunting
Sage and Secrets
Patchouli and Problems
Angelica and an Awful End

Prequel: Hemlock and Hedge

A REVIEW IS WORTH ITS WEIGHT IN GOLD!

I really hope you enjoyed reading this story. I was wondering if you could spare a couple of moments to rate and review this book? As an indie author, one of the best ways you can help support my dream of being an author is to leave me a review on your favourite online book store, or even tell your friends.

Reviews help other readers, just like you, to take a chance on a new writer!

Thank you!
Silver Nord

ALSO BY SILVER NORD

JANUARY CHEVALIER SUPERNATURAL MYSTERIES

Death's Dark Horse

Death's Hexed Hobnobs

Death's Endless Enchanter

Death's Ethereal Enemy

Death's Last Laugh

Prequel: Death's Reckless Reaper

Printed in Great Britain
by Amazon